Da

D.J. and Alfred stopped in their tracks, flashing their lights in the direction the dogs were looking. Whatever the dogs saw seemed to be hidden in the darkness just beyond a ponderosa tree trunk that had crashed in a windstorm.

"Something's moving over there! What do you think it is, D.J.?" Alfred asked, holding the light on the branches of the fallen tree.

"Let's go find out, Alfred."

Cautiously, the boys moved ahead. As they carefully peered over the big log, a pair of eyes suddenly shone in their flashlights. "There!" D.J. cried. "Close to the ground!"

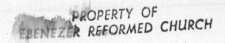

LEE RODDY is a former staff writer and researcher for a movie production company. He lives in the Sierra Nevada Mountains of California and devotes his time to writing books and public speaking. He is a co-writer of the book which became the TV series, "The Life and Times of Grizzly Adams."

Born on an Illinois farm and reared on a California ranch, Lee Roddy grew up around hunters and trail hounds. As a boy, he began writing animal stories. He spent lots of time reading about dogs, horses, and other animals. These stories shaped his thinking and values before he went to Hollywood to write professionally. His Christian commitment later turned his writing talents to books like this one. This is the sixth book in the D.J. Dillon Adventure Series.

The Legend of the White Raccoon

LEE RODDY

VICTOR BOOKS™

A DIVISION OF SCRIPTURE PRESS PUBLICATIONS INC.
USA CANADA ENGLAND

Scripture quotations are from the *King James Version.*

Library of Congress Catalog Card Number: 86-60972
ISBN: 0-89693-500-0

VICTOR BOOKS
A division of SP Publications, Inc.
.   Wheaton, Illinois 60187

CONTENTS

To
Merrill J. Alexander, M.D.
A Bible study partner
who made a difference
in this life and
the one to come

Chapter One

THE MYSTERIOUS STRANGERS

It didn't seem like the kind of a night that would plunge D.J. Dillon into terrible danger. He and his best friend, Alfred Milford, were just out hunting without weapons when it started.

The full moon of early November shone coldly down from above the rugged granite peaks of California's Sierra Nevada Mountains. Devil's Slide Canyon was filled with spooky shadows. The boys ran along a narrow deer trail that followed the bank of Mad River. The boys were following the distant sound of their dogs. They'd just struck a game trail and were making the mountains echo with their deep voices.

As the friends rounded a small rock outcropping, they heard a strange sound just ahead. Both boys slid to a stop on the fallen pine needles and oak leaves.

"What was that?" D.J. demanded, trying to

7

control his breathing so he could hear better. He flipped his five-cell flashlight's powerful beam around.

"Don't know," Alfred admitted. He used his right thumb to push up the thick glasses that slid down his nose. He turned in his boot tracks, flicking his three-cell flashlight over the dense underbrush. The light showed only stately ponderosas,* a couple of sugar pines,* and a huge black oak with golden leaves. The boys' breath made little puffy explosions in the crisp air.

An owl whirred by on silent wings, then screeched just above the boys' heads. Instinctively, both boys ducked.

"Wow!" D.J. exclaimed, catching the big bird for a moment in the flashlight's beam. "It sounded like he was going to land on my cap!"

Alfred leaned against a huge fallen Douglas fir and clutched his side. "Owls won't hurt you. Guess that's what we heard. Boy! My side aches from running so hard."

D.J. forgot about the strange sound. "What'd you suppose Hero and Bugler are chasing?" he asked, cocking his head to hear better.

Alfred unbuttoned an old navy pea coat his father had picked up at a thrift shop someplace. "Doesn't matter. We're not going to take anything; just have fun."

"Yeah," D.J. agreed, sitting on the fallen log beside his friend. D.J. brushed his yellowish hair away from his blue eyes. He had always hunted with a gun until Kathy Stagg moved to Stoney Ridge. She

*You can find an explanation of the starred words under "Life in Stoney Ridge" on pages 114-118.

didn't like any wild creature hurt, and slowly D.J.
had given up hunting like other mountain boys. Alfred
just liked to be with D.J., so it didn't matter if neither
boy carried a weapon.

A rifle safety clicked into place. D.J. and Alfred
leaped up, flipping their flashlights into the brush
beside the river. D.J.'s heart leaped into a panicky
gallop.

A strange kid stood blinking in the flashlights'
beams. D.J. and Alfred knew everyone in this part of
the mountains, but not this boy.

He was about thirteen, the same as D.J. But this
stranger was more solidly built than D.J. The
newcomer had long, straight black hair that hadn't
been cut in a couple years. The hair fell from under a
long-billed cap. A miner's old carbide* lamp
glistened copper-colored above his forehead. The boy
wore faded and patched overalls and knee length
laced leather boots.

"Did . . . did you see him?" the boy asked almost
in a whisper. He moved forward, an old single shot
twenty-two rifle cradled in his arms. He used his
right hand to shade his eyes from the flashlights.

"See who?" D.J. asked, feeling his heart slowing
down. Neither he nor Alfred had even sensed that this
stranger was anywhere near.

"The white 'coon!" the boy said as he swung his
head off to the right and motioned with his right hand.
"He was right there on that bull pine!"*

"White 'coon?" D.J. asked, flashing his light
around the area where the kid had pointed. "You
mean a raccoon? A ringtail?"

"Yes, except he was *white!*" The kid's voice was

almost a whisper. "*Pure* white! Didn't you see him?"

D.J. and Alfred exchanged glances. They both flicked their flashlights around the conifers* but there were no reflected animal eyes. There was no sound except the river flowing over a riffle and a slight sigh as the night winds played through the needles at the very top of the trees. Far away, D.J. could hear his dog, Hero, and Alfred's hound warming up a trail.

For a long moment, none of the three boys said anything. They turned their eyes upward, following the flashlights' beams from limb to limb. Slowly, the lights moved down to the brush and then to the river a few feet away. Ghost-like fog vapors rose from the backwaters of Mad River.

The mountain air was sharp at the 3,500-foot elevation, and sound carried well. Yet a moment ago D.J. wouldn't have guessed there was another person in the whole canyon area.

The strange boy turned to look at D.J. and Alfred. "Sky will *have* to have that white 'coon!"

D.J. saw the stranger's eyes were a very pale blue. He rubbed his right hand across his nose. The stranger's forehead was wide under the miner's cap.

The kid went on. "I know you'll want that 'coon too, but he'll whip me good if anybody takes him except'n me'n him."

D.J. asked, "Who's Sky?"

"He's the man I—I live with. Real name's Skiver; Durant Skiver, but he's called Sky. Well, he likes me to call him 'Pap' for Pappy, though he ain't really my father or no kin to me."

The boy glanced off into the dense trees. D.J. automatically flipped his light that way. The deer trail showed through the underbrush by the river.

The stranger continued, "But he makes me call him *Pap* in front of people. I do too, 'cause he's a mean one to fight and whips me purty good now and then when he's mad. So I sure hope you'ns know I'd take it kindly if you didn't beat us to catchin' that there white 'coon!"

D.J. hadn't heard a kid talk the way this boy did in a long time. Some of the older folks in town did talk that way. A few of the younger loggers and mountain people around Stoney Ridge also talked different from what the teachers told them was proper, but not quite like this kid.

D.J. asked, "You new around here?"

The strange kid started to nod, but Alfred interrupted.

"What about the white 'coon? I've heard the legend, of course, but I always thought it was just a story. You *sure* you saw him?"

"Sure did!" The stranger turned his head. "Right over yonder! Plain as day! But white as could be! Got me so excited I liked to of quit breathing, purt' near! Then I heard you two coming so I turned off my lamp and hid. Sky don't cotton much to me talkin' to strangers."

"Hey!" A man's voice exploded from the darkness behind D.J. like a bellow from an angry bull. "Who are you kids? What're you doing bothering my boy?"

The man came out of the night without a sound, his feet making no noise on the fallen leaves and pine needles. D.J. swallowed hard and turned with Alfred, automatically swinging up their flashlights.

"Get them lights off'n me!" The voice hit again

from the night, hard as a pick handle.

D.J. and Alfred obeyed. It took a moment for their eyes to adjust to the night. There was enough moonlight that D.J. could see a man moving toward them from a stand of young ponderosa. He wasn't as big as Brother Paul, Stoney Ridge's lay pastor, but this man was big. He looked to D.J. as if part of the night had broken off and was walking toward him.

The strange kid spoke softly. "I'm sorry, Pap, but I seen the white 'coon, and we just stopped to. . . . "

"Shut up, Cletus!" The man's voice was so strong it echoed off the mountainsides. "Now you two kids—hear me and hear me good! I keep my boy to home and I want your dads to do the same! You hear?"

D.J. managed to swallow hard and reply weakly. "Yes."

Alfred echoed the same word, adding softly, "Sir."

The voice cracked again. "I catch you hangin' around this here boy of mine again and you'll wisht you was never borned! Now git!"

D.J. and Alfred backed up a few steps, then turned and snapped their lights on.

The man's angry voice hit them from behind. "Git, I say!"

The two friends bolted into the night, back the way they had come, their dogs forgotten. But behind them they heard a sharp slap and a cry from the kid.

"Don't, Pap! I didn't do nothin'!"

"You talk too much!"

Then the voices were drowned out by the river gushing over boulders.

D.J. felt tears in his eyes as he ran. He wasn't sure it was from fear now turning to anger, or from the cold wind slicing through the canyon.

Alfred puffed, "Makes me mad! Who's he think he is, anyway?"

D.J. didn't answer. He kept running through the brush, following a faint deer trail by flashlight. But in that moment, D.J. hoped he would never again run into that man, whoever he was.

D.J. also knew something else. He turned to glance at his friend. "No matter if it's the last thing we ever do, Alfred, we've got to find that white 'coon before that man does!"

Alfred groaned. "I wish you hadn't said it that way!"

D.J. barely whispered his thoughts. "Me too!"

Chapter Two

SOMETIMES NOTHING GOES RIGHT

D.J. awoke the next morning to the sound of raised voices. He opened his eyes but didn't really see the ceiling. He moaned, rolled over, and pulled the pillow over his head.

"Oh, no! Not again!"

From the kitchen down the hallway, the mountain boy could hear his father's voice. It was firm but controlled. Even under the pillow, D.J. knew from the tone that Dad was not giving in.

The woman's reply was higher, less controlled. D.J.'s stepmother, whom he called Two Mom, was trying to keep her voice down, but the boy caught her words.

"It's difficult enough for a stepfamily to make adjustments, Sam! But three generations under one roof is too much! I'm sorry, but that old man is driving me out of my mind!"

Dad's voice was louder, sharper. "Careful,

Hannah! That's *my father* you're talking about!"

"And he's a wonderful man, Sam! As a Christian wife and mother, I'm trying to love him, but it's just not working out! He and Priscilla got into it again last night over nothing! She cried herself to sleep! Then he and I tangled over that! You got home late and missed it all!"

The voices dropped again and the boy couldn't hear any more. Pris was his nine-year-old stepsister. D.J. had always had problems with her even before his mother died and Dad married Pris' widowed mother last April.

The boy sighed and folded his hands across his chest.

"Why, Lord?" he whispered. "Two Mom's a good stepmother, but she can't throw Grandpa out! I love him!"

When D.J. heard the back door close and Dad's car start, the boy got out of bed. He went to the bathroom and slapped his hands to his forehead. "Oh, no! Not again!" he cried.

He stepped back into the hallway to complain to his stepmother because Pris had left the bathroom a mess again. But D.J. decided not to say anything. Pris had probably been in a hurry because she was going on a school field trip early today.

However, this annoyance was made worse because D.J. was still upset over the strange man running him and Alfred out of the woods the night before. It was easy for D.J. to let himself become angry now. He tried to fight the feeling, but it wasn't easy.

He dressed quickly, working around his step-sister's soggy towels thrown on the floor with her pajamas. D.J. was in a sour mood when he walked down the hallway to the kitchen.

Two Mom was a slightly plump woman with blond hair. She turned from the sink where she'd been washing the breakfast dishes. "You got in pretty late last night, D.J."

There was still a sharp edge to her tone. The boy frowned, annoyed. He didn't answer, but got a bowl and cold cereal from the cupboard and a half-gallon milk carton from the refrigerator. He carried them to the small kitchen table with the formica top and sat down heavily in a chrome chair.

"Are you upset, D.J.?" Two Mom asked, her tone softer.

"I heard you and Dad talking about throwing Grandpa out!"

He hadn't meant to say it that way, but it popped out.

"D.J., it's not that way at all! Please try to understand! After your mother was killed, your grandfather became the cook and housekeeper in your old house. He's used to running a home. But that's *my* responsibility in this house."

D.J. interrupted. "Sometimes I wish we had that old house back!"

His stepmother stopped washing a dish and stood very still for a moment. Softly, she said, "That's what Grandpa Dillon said last night. He said he'd like to live there again. Oh, D.J., we're trying to be a Christian family! Let's not allow anything to tear us apart!"

D.J. stared glumly at the milk carton. He didn't really see the photo of the missing child on the side panel.

"Where's Grandpa?" he asked, pushing back his
chair. He'd want to know about the white raccoon.

"He went for a walk early, but I think I hear his
old rocker squeaking on the front porch."

The boy started out of the room. Two Mom called
after him. "Aren't you going to eat breakfast?"

"I'm not hungry."

"Then please put everything away!"

D.J. obeyed in silence, then stalked through the
house toward the front door. He grabbed his heavy
jacket from a peg behind the door and stepped onto
the porch.

Grandpa Dillon was staring into the tree-lined
street of Stoney Ridge. His skinny right hand held a
cane. He wore wire-rimmed bifocals, faded blue
jeans, and an old fedora hat. His thin shoulders were
hunched up inside a checked brown and tan
overcoat with a turned up fur collar. It covered his chin
so only his cheeks were exposed to the cold.

He was a feisty little man who had become a
Christian just a short time before. But he was still
having trouble with his old nature.

He was rocking hard. D.J. knew what that meant:
Grandpa was upset, and soon he'd rock too hard and
tip over backward. Sometimes it was almost
humorous because the old man never hurt himself
when the chair went over. But nothing was funny to
D.J. this morning.

"Careful, Grandpa!" the boy called, trying to
sound cheerful. "You'll tip over again!" D.J. warned as
he pulled on his warm coat and zipped it up. He
took his stocking cap out of the jacket's right front
pocket and put it on.

Grandpa's chair rocked very far forward, then way back. This time it didn't come forward again. Instead, it teetered a moment on the back point of the rockers. Then the chair eased on over backward.

D.J. tried to grab the rocker, but it was too late. Grandpa Dillon sailed awkwardly through the air like a half-filled gunny sack. His arms flailed wildly as he tried to catch himself. He held onto the old cane he called his Irish shillelagh.* He landed on the wooden porch floor beside the chair.

"Now, Grandpa!" D.J. cried, but the old man didn't seem to hear.

Grandpa rolled over on his left side and raised the blackthorn walking stick above his head. He began whacking the fallen red chair. The wicker bottom made snapping sounds as the blows fell hard.

D.J. waited until the old man stopped flailing away. Silently, the boy reached down and helped Grandpa to his feet. D.J. righted the chair and Grandpa started to sit down again. He used the cane to help ease himself down so his arthritic hip wouldn't hurt him.

"D.J., I done it again! Plumb let Ol' Nick* get to me!"

"It's OK, Grandpa." D.J. sat down at the old man's feet and looked up at him. Grandpa's blue eyes were sad and there might have been a hint of tears in the corners.

"No, it's not, D.J.! A man who's walking with the Lord shouldn't get so upset when things don't go right!"

D.J. pursed his lips thoughtfully. "I heard Dad and Two Mom talking this morning while you were out walking. You really planning to find a place of your own?"

"Wisht I could have our old house back! The one that burned down across the creek. Remember?"

Slowly, D.J. took a deep breath. "I remember," he said softly. He added, "Lots of memories in that old house."

The Dillons had lived there for years. In the summertime, D.J. always took off his shoes at the side of the paved country road and waded the creek.

In the winter, he had to walk upstream quite a distance to cross some twelve-by-twelve planks. Dad used to drive his pickup through the creek, across the stoney bottom, and up the slick unpaved ruts toward the house.

D.J. had lived there with his parents and Grandpa when Mr. Higgins, Two Mom's first husband, had been killed in a logging accident. D.J. was living there when his mother died in an auto accident. He'd lived there when he'd gotten Hero, his hair-pulling bear dog,* and when he met Alfred.

Grandpa spoke softly, reaching down to touch D.J.'s still-damp hair. "The Good Book says that when a man marries, he should leave his father and mother and cleave only unto his wife. Well, I reckon that means—in my case, anyway—that *I* should do the leaving."

D.J. was sad. "Where'll you go, Grandpa?"

"Don't rightly know yet. But I'm a'thinking and a'praying on it."

"I'd like to go with you, Grandpa."

The old man's hand seemed to shake a moment on the boy's head. "Now, D.J., I know it's hard making adjustments to a stepfamily, but it's got to be done. Your place is here—with your father, his new wife, and your new sister."

D.J. had tried to believe that, but it wasn't what he wanted to hear right now. He decided to change the subject.

"Grandpa, you ever hear a legend about a white raccoon?"

The old man chuckled and removed his hand from the boy's head. Grandpa pounded the rubber tip of his cane onto the porch. "Everybody's heard that story a hundred times, D.J. Lots of fools believe it's true."

D.J. slowly got to his feet. "You don't believe it?"

"Not for nary a minute, I don't!"

The boy turned to look thoughtfully toward the street. Their house sat on the side of a hill overlooking the small mountain community of Stoney Ridge. Some slender liquidambar* trees were beautiful with red and gold leaves. A spreading red maple seemed almost to glow in the morning sun. Above them, conifers soared as tall as a five-story building.

"Grandpa," D.J. said softly, turning back around, "Alfred and I ran into a kid last night out hunting. He said he saw that white 'coon."

Grandpa cackled like a Rhode Island hen that had just laid an egg. "Did *you* see that ringtail, D.J.?"

"No."

"Did Alfred?"

"No."

"There's your answer!" Grandpa leaned back triumphantly and began rocking slowly. "Ain't no such critter!"

D.J. didn't want to believe that. "This kid seemed awful sincere and honest, Grandpa."

"You know this kid?"

"No. Never saw him before."

"A stranger, eh? D.J., 'pears to me you've been hornswaggled."*

D.J. frowned. He decided to tell Grandpa about the mean-tempered man. Grandpa listened without comment until the boy had finished telling about the whole experience last night.

"Well, now, D.J., that sounds like the kind of man to steer clear of. But nothing you said makes me believe any different about the kid. I don't think he seen any such thing as a white 'coon cause there ain't no such animal! It's a story; a legend, as you said."

D.J. was thoughtful a long time. He turned to look again across the town, seeing the steeple of the little church rising above every other man-made thing.

"Grandpa, what if it's really *true*, and there is such an animal as that kid said he saw?"

The old man snorted, but nodded. "Just for the sake of argument, let's say there is. What do you want to know next?"

"Would that animal be valuable?"

"Bring a pretty penny, you can be sure! Why, some people would give their eyeteeth* to see such a critter up close!"

"Suppose I could catch it?"

Grandpa cackled again. "Brother Paul's red-headed girl would plumb skin you alive!"

D.J. swallowed a little uncomfortably. Ever since Kathy Stagg had moved into Stoney Ridge, he'd had nothing but trouble with her. She was the one who'd

convinced him to catch Ol' Satchelfoot, the outlaw
bear, have his sore jaw treated, and then release the
bear in the high country. With the help of her father,
the town's lay preacher, D.J. had done that.

D.J. couldn't explain why that girl had such an in-
fluence on him, especially since they always seemed to
take opposite sides on everything.

Grandpa was grinning like a cat that had just
found a whole saucer of cream with nobody around to
stop him from enjoying it. "Whether that there white
'coon is real or not, D.J., you'd better count on having
your hands full with that redheaded girl if you even
talk about going after such a wild animal."

D.J. sighed. Nothing was going right! D.J. decided that it wouldn't hurt to ask Brother Paul what *he*
thought about the legend of the white raccoon.

"Grandpa, I'm going to walk over to the Staggs'
place."

"To talk with Brother Paul about that white 'coon,
or to see his daughter?" Grandpa's voice was teasing.

"Ah, Grandpa! To see Brother Paul, of course!"

Grandpa grinned broadly. " 'Course you are, D.J.!
'Course you are!"

The boy walked down to the sidewalk and headed
across town. He felt hot around the ears and wasn't
quite sure why. *Maybe,* he told himself, *no matter
what I say, Kathy's going to find some reason to get
riled at me! Well, that white 'coon's worth it!*

Chapter Three

KATHY CHALLENGES D.J.

D.J.'s heart was beating hard when he finished
climbing the hill to the small frame house where the
Paul Stagg family lived. The boy had decided what
to say to keep from getting into a spirited discussion
with Kathy Stagg.

She opened the screen door. At thirteen, she was
very slender and taller than any boy in her class except
D.J. Her blue eyes lit up as she smiled.

"You're out early, D.J.," she said. Her reddish
hair, parted in the middle, rippled down both sides of
her face and brushed her shoulders. She wore blue
jeans and an old white blouse. Her face and bare arms
were covered with freckles.

The mountain boy swallowed before answering.
"Hi, Kathy. Your father around?"

"Around in back, splitting firewood."

"Thanks." D.J. turned to go down the steps, then

hesitated. He was a little self-conscious around
Kathy. He wanted to get along with her. He would
have liked to tease her. She had qualities he liked.
She wasn't bossy like his stepsister, but she was
spirited. She had her own opinions, especially about
environmental issues. Too often D.J. and Kathy
disagreed. He knew she wouldn't like him even
thinking about trapping the white raccoon. However,
on the walk up the hill, D.J. had planned how he'd
handle that.

Kathy interrupted his thoughts, "Something
wrong?"

"No, no! I was just thinking about something." He
started down the stairs, but turned back to look up at
her. "You ever hear about a white raccoon?"

She shook her head slowly. "No. Why?"

"Alfred and I met a kid last night who said he saw
one."

"Well, I suppose there could be such an animal.
I've read about such things. They're called albinos.
Plants and animals and even people can be albinos.
It has something to do with not having certain
pigment* in their skins. Albinos usually have pink
eyes too."

D.J. nodded. He had often seen white rabbits with
pink eyes.

"I'll go ask your father if he thinks it's possible for
a white raccoon to live in these mountains."

" 'Bye," she said, smiling.

"See you later," he answered and went around the
side of the house.

Paul Stagg was using an eight-pound maul* to
drive a long metal wedge into the end of a foot-thick

chunk of oak firewood. The ring of metal on metal
as the maul fell was followed by the sound of
hardwood slowly splitting open.

Brother Paul was about the biggest man D.J. had
ever seen. Stoney Ridge's lay preacher was at least six
feet, four inches tall, D.J. figured. He wore polished
saddle-colored cowboy boots, blue jeans, a wide belt
buckle with a bucking horse embossed on it, and a
cowboy shirt with horseshoes embroidered above the
pockets. He had taken off his jacket so he could
move more easily.

His white ten-gallon Stetson* made him look
closer to seven feet tall. The hat slid down over Paul
Stagg's eyes as the maul flashed through the air and
connected squarely with the wedge. The wood parted
cleanly and the big man stepped back with
satisfaction.

"Morning, D.J.," Brother Paul said as he turned to
grin at his visitor. The big man's voice seemed to come
from deep inside his big chest, making a pleasant
rumbling sound. "I was just fixing to take a break. Set
one of those rounds on end and seat yourself."

As D.J. obeyed, the woodcutter perched himself
on a cord* of wood already stacked. Brother Paul
removed his hat and hooked it over the toe of his
right boot. His reddish hair was damp from
perspiration. He rubbed the back of his huge right
hand over his forehead and exclaimed, "Whew! That's
warming work!"

"Sure is," D.J. agreed. He had been splitting
firewood since he could remember.

"What brings you out so early on a Saturday
morning, D.J.? I'd expect you'd sleep in."

"Too excited, I guess."

"What about?"

"Well," he began, and told about his and Alfred Milford's experiences the night before, and the fact that neither of the boys had ever seen Cletus in school. D.J. ended with the question he had come to ask.

"Brother Paul, Grandpa says that there isn't any such animal; that white 'coons are just a legend; a story people tell. Is that true?"

The big man thoughtfully juggled his hat on the end of his boot. "To be right truthful, D.J., I don't know about that. Yet, I've hunted about all the animals that live. Well, I did until Kathy got interested in conservation and started making so much fuss I quit hunting for sport."

D.J. tried not to sound disappointed. "Then you never heard of a white raccoon?"

"No, not really. But I've heard tell of plenty of other white animals. On TV one night I saw a couple of white tigers. Once I heard of a big buck—a deer—that was pure white. And when I was a boy in Oklahoma, I heard tell about how Indians thought a white buffalo was some kind of spirit. But I never heard tell of a white raccoon."

"But there could be such an animal?" D.J. persisted.

"I suppose so. There's an awful lot of what they call 'primitive area' around here. Bound to be creatures in those hills nobody's seen."

He snapped his fingers. "Say, D.J., come to think of it, awhile back I *did* hear a couple of old men sitting in front of the general store talking about a story about a white raccoon. Seems they'd seen this animal around here when they were boys. And if I remember right, they claimed their fathers had seen this 'coon too. But I thought they were just talking to pass the time, so I didn't really pay too much attention."

The boy asked doggedly, "If it was true, would that animal be valuable?"

Brother Paul nodded. "Mighty valuable, I'd say. Circuses or zoos would pay plenty, I suppose. Why? You thinking of trapping that 'coon?"

"Yes, Brother Paul, but not to keep. I'd do it to stop that animal from being trapped or killed by that mean-talking man Alfred and I met last night."

"What would you do with it?"

"I'd have Alfred take pictures and I'd write a story for the Indian Springs newspaper where I'm a stringer.* Since I'm going to be a writer someday, maybe I'll even sell the story to one of those outdoor magazines. I hear they pay for such things. Then I'd turn the raccoon loose again."

"Need some money, do you?"

"Well, Grandpa's been wanting to move out into his own place again, but he doesn't have much money. He could have what I get paid for the 'coon story."

"Yes, I know. He came by awhile ago and asked me to help him find a place."

"He wants that old house back we had when Mom died. But it burned down, you know."

"I remember, D.J. But it just so happens I know the man who built that house. It wasn't very fancy, so maybe he could rebuild it. That's what Grandpa Dillon asked me to find out about."

D.J. frowned. "But he'd be all alone! No phone, no

near neighbors—no nothing! It wouldn't be like when we all lived there before Mom got killed."

"Your grandfather told me he thought he could get a companion to live with him."

The boy shook his head. "Grandpa's not the easiest person to get along with, even if he *is* a Christian now and trying to live for the Lord."

"Well, if it's right, the Lord will provide a companion for Brother Dillon. Now, let's get back to the white raccoon. You know, it's not too likely an animal like that would survive."

"Oh? Why not?"

"Lots of reasons. God made most creatures with some kind of natural coloring that blends in with their surroundings. It's called camouflage. Makes them harder to see. A white raccoon wouldn't have any such protection, so his chances of getting killed would be greater."

"But if he's a very smart animal—and all 'coons are pretty smart, I hear—wouldn't that help?"

The big man chuckled. "He'd have to be a powerfully smart critter, D.J. But yes—if he survived for any length of time, he'd probably be about the smartest 'coon around. That would naturally make him much harder to catch too."

The boy nodded thoughtfully. "If there was such an animal, and what those old men said was true, then this white raccoon would be over a hundred years old."

Brother Paul laughed pleasantly. "My guess is that—if there is such a 'coon—there have been several generations, all white. There's just no way one raccoon could live that long."

"Could it be something that's passed on from one generation to another—being all white, I mean—like people's kids look like their parents with blue eyes or brown or whatever?"

"You got me there, D.J.! I'm just a plain ol' country preacher—and a lay preacher at that—and I don't rightly know about such things. Why don't you ask your friend, Alfred? I hear tell all the kids at school call him 'The Brain.' "

D.J. picked up a chunk of pink-colored madrone* wood and idly rolled it between his palms. "He doesn't like to be called that. But he said last night he'd go read up on raccoons today. He's got an old set of encyclopedias his mother bought him at a garage sale."

"Well, D.J., now that you know what little bit I've heard about white animals, what're you going to do about the raccoon you heard about last night?"

Before he could answer, D.J. saw Kathy coming out the back door with a metal tray and two steaming white cups.

"Mom says you two might like some hot cocoa."

D.J. and Brother Paul took the hot mugs and thanked her. She perched on the end of the stacked wood with her father.

"Well," she asked, glancing from the boy to her father, "what about the white raccoon?"

D.J. repeated what he'd learned. Brother Paul nodded.

Kathy asked, "I got to thinking, D.J. Are you planning on bothering that animal?"

The boy felt his insides twist. "I wouldn't hurt it, Kathy. Grandpa could help me fix up a harmless box

trap. That's better than having someone kill it
or. . . . "

The girl interrupted. "Then you *are* going to trap
it!"

Before D.J. could answer, Brother Paul's deep
voice interrupted.

"Kathy, think about it this way: What if D.J.
caught that white raccoon in some safe way so it
wouldn't get hurt—like with Ol' Satchelfoot, the
bear—and took it up in the higher elevations
someplace and turned it loose? Wouldn't that be
better than letting that stranger kill the raccoon or sell
it to a zoo?"

Kathy turned her blue eyes on D.J. and stared
deeply in his. "Is that what you'd do, D.J.?"

"Well," he said, taking a sip of the cocoa and
thinking fast, "I really don't want another pet. I've had
a bear, and I've got my dog, Hero. Besides, my
stepmother's allergic to animals. I'm lucky she lets me
keep Hero."

Kathy looked steadily into the boy's eyes. "You
wouldn't hurt the 'coon? You'd let him loose?"

D.J. nodded, smiling at the girl. Maybe they
weren't going to get into a disagreement this time.

"Then," Kathy said, jumping off the stack of
firewood, "I suppose it'd be OK."

Her father chuckled. "I guess that settles it, D.J.!
You've got to catch that white raccoon for his own
good!"

Kathy took the empty cup from her father and
reached for D.J.'s. She asked, "But what if it turns out
there really is no such animal? It might just be a
legend, after all!"

"If it's real," D.J. said quietly, "I'll catch it."

Brother Paul retrieved his hat from his boot toe
and stood up. He reached over and laid a huge hand
gently on the boy's shoulder. "You watch out for that
mean stranger! He might hurt you and Alfred."

"We'll be careful," D.J. replied.

Kathy frowned. "What are you talking about,
Dad?"

"I'll tell you later, Dear. Well, I'd better finish
splitting this wood. Keep me posted on things, D.J."

"I will," he promised. He waved to the father and
daughter and walked briskly around the house and
down the hill.

He felt uneasy about the mean-sounding stranger
who'd warned him last night. D.J. didn't want any
trouble, but he had a right to hunt that white raccoon. All D.J. had to do was stay away from the new
kid. For a friendly boy like D.J. Dillon, that wasn't
going to be easy.

Especially, he thought as he hurried along, kicking fallen leaves off the high sidewalk, *if there's a mystery involved. And there's sure something mysterious about that kid and that man! Alfred and I will
find out what it is!*

And that, D.J. knew, could mean plenty of trouble!

Chapter Four

DANGER FROM A POACHER'S TRAP

D.J. and Alfred chose to explore a little before deciding how to best trap the white raccoon—if it was real. By early evening, the boys were already scrambling down the steep trail into the remote wilderness area of Devil's Slide Canyon. Mad River ran along the canyon bottom.

The autumn wind was sharp that night. It seemed to slice through the heavy old woolen jacket D.J. wore. But the excitement of hunting the white raccoon kept D.J.'s blood flowing. He felt warm.

His dog, Hero, was anxious to be off the leash and hunting. The scruffy mutt and Alfred's hound, Bugler, had come in on their own after the boys had been run out of the canyon by Durant Skiver. Now Hero sniffed loudly, testing the night air. He pulled so hard against his chain leash that he sometimes gasped.

"If you wouldn't pull so hard, you wouldn't choke

32

yourself," D.J. scolded. "Now, come back here at the proper heel position. Heel, I say." He jerked sharply on the leash. The dog reluctantly obeyed.

Hero was what bear hunters called a "hair-puller," "cut-across," or "heeler." Big game like bears are trailed by hounds, like Bugler, a black and tan, that follow a scent trail. When the game is treed,* or brought to bay by the hounds, the crossbreed hair-puller is turned loose. He instinctively goes for the prey's hindquarters. Hounds tend to go for the quarry's forequarters where it's more dangerous. By having hounds and dogs working at both ends of their prey, the animals were less likely to be hurt.

While a raccoon is a relatively small animal, he's a powerful fighter that sometimes can kill a dog. D.J. and Alfred didn't intend to have their dogs attack the white raccoon, but that didn't mean the animal might not defend himself against the dogs.

Hero was half hound, part Australian Shepherd, and only one-fourth Airedale. He was reddish-brown, with shaggy hair and a stub tail. He had a long, funny black nose that stuck out from his muzzle like a plum on a thumb.

Alfred was also having trouble controlling his black and tan hound. Bugler had come to the Milford home as a skinny stray with very sore pads. At first, Alfred had called the hound Blackie. But after the experiences with the "ghost dog" of Stoney Ridge, Alfred changed the hound's name to Bugler.

Bugler was a "loner," a hound that wouldn't run a trail with another dog. Once Bugler had struck a scent and was closing in on the game, he would let other dogs join him for the final chase and baying treed.

D.J. glanced at the sky. The moon was high above the canyon walls, seeming to touch the very tip of a fifteen-story tall sugar pine. The glowing moon looked like a lighted ornament on a Christmas tree.

"You scared, D.J.?" Alfred asked, pulling his stocking cap down farther over his ears.

"Why should I be scared?"

"You know! That guy—Sky—threatened us last night. He could be hiding out here waiting for us."

"He *could,* but I doubt it. This area of the river belongs to the government, so anybody can use it. That guy's got no right to run us off."

"I don't think he cares much about rights. Sky never lets that boy go to school—at least, not to Stoney Ridge—And I doubt that he goes to Indian Springs School either." Alfred stopped and used his right thumb to push his thick glasses farther up on his nose. "You suppose there are any bears around here?"

"The mountains are full of them, but they're not close or the dogs would've smelled them."

"Yeah, you're right. Say, isn't this about where we saw that new kid last night?"

D.J. flashed his light around the area. "Sure is! There's the tree he said the white raccoon was in."

Alfred bent over his hound's head. "Let's turn Bugler loose and see if he picks up that 'coon's trail."

The flop-eared black and tan was soon smashing through the underbrush, sniffing loudly. The boys kept their flashlights on Bugler. His heavy tail swung noisily against the brush. Suddenly, the hound stopped dead still.

At the same instant, Hero tensed on his leash. D.J. and Alfred stopped in their tracks, flashing their lights

in the direction the dogs were looking. Whatever the
dogs saw seemed to be hidden in the darkness just
beyond a ponderosa tree trunk that had crashed in a
windstorm.

D.J. heard something move in the brush beyond
the log. Hero heard it too. He barked suddenly,
sharply. For such a little dog, he had the loudest
bark D.J. had ever heard.

"Something's moving over there! What do you
think it is, D.J.?" Alfred asked, holding the light on the
branches of the fallen tree.

"Let's go find out, Alfred."

His friend groaned. "I was afraid you'd say that."

"Well, it's not a bear or mountain lion or anything
like that," D.J. answered. "See? The dogs have lost
interest."

"Must be 'trash,' " Alfred agreed. He meant deer,
coyote, and other animals that weren't hunted by dogs.

Cautiously, the boys moved ahead, still holding
Hero's leash. Bugler moved off into the night, cutting
back and forth in the brush, smelling for a game
scent.

As the boys carefully peered over the big log, a
pair of eyes suddenly shone in their flashlights.
"There!" D.J. cried. "Close to the ground!"

"A deer!" Alfred exclaimed. He let his breath out
so hard it made a white puff in the crisp night air.
"Why is she just laying there on her side like that?
Why doesn't she run?"

A moment later, the boys saw the answer. The doe
was nearly strangled to death from a noose around her
slender neck.

"A poacher!" D.J. exclaimed. "Somebody's set a

snare! That's against the law! Come on! Let's see if we can free her."

Hero trotted up and sniffed the stricken deer. She struggled violently, choking and gasping. The snare was made to pull tighter with every move the animal made. D.J. ordered his dog away from the suffering deer.

"Hurry!" D.J. cried, pulling off his heavy coat. "Maybe we can still save her!"

He came up on her from behind, away from her tiny thrashing black hooves. They could slice a person's flesh to ribbons. D.J. threw his jacket over the female's front hooves. Alfred did the same with the hind feet. The deer was gasping weakly for air as D.J. bent over her shoulder. While Alfred tried to keep the coats on the animal's legs, D.J. set his light on the ground so he could use both hands to loosen the killing noose.

He got it loosened enough so that the deer's terrible gasping sounds stopped. She was too weak to move. She noisily sucked air into her lungs. In another moment, D.J. worked the snare over the nearly-dead animal's head.

"There!" D.J. threw the noose free. It sailed away in a thin, silvery arc to vanish into the night. D.J.grabbed his coat from her hooves and jumped back. "Get clear! Let's see if she's able to get up."

Alfred retrieved his coat and leaped back. Both boys held their flashlights on the doe. For a moment, the exhausted animal lay on her side, breathing hard, getting back the breath the strong snare had cut off.

Then, with a toss of her dainty head, the doe

struggled to her feet. She stood uncertainly, swaying on widespread feet. Her soft eyes rolled wildly as she watched the boys. Then her long ears shot up and she staggered weakly into the underbrush.

"Good girl!" D.J. called after her.

Alfred used his flashlight to find the noose. Then he walked into the forest to where the snare lay coiled in the underbrush. He examined it with his light. "Piano wire, maybe," he said softly. "The other end's tied around that log. Who'd be mean enough to do a thing like that?"

D.J. looked at his friend. Through the soft glow of their flashlights, both knew the answer.

"That man we met last night!" D.J. exclaimed softly. "Not the boy—but Sky!"

Alfred worked the other end of the snare loose from the tree trunk. "That's a terrible way for an animal to die."

"Sure is!" D.J. agreed. "That wire's strong enough to catch a person too." He flashed his light around, then stopped it abruptly. "Oh no! There's another snare over there!"

The light reflected off a thin strand of silvery-colored wire. One end was attached to a young ponderosa pine that had been bent nearly double. The other end wasn't visible in the fallen leaves and needles.

"Keep Hero away!" D.J. said. "I'll spring this trap!"

He picked up a four-foot length of fallen limb from the downed ponderosa. D.J. dragged the end of the limb across the leaves where he figured the "set" was hidden. The limb was suddenly jerked from his hand. The supple young pine tree snapped upright. The piece of dead limb bounced crazily in the air from the end of the piano wire snare.

"Wow!" Alfred exclaimed. "If one of us had stepped in that thing, we'd be hanging upside down in the air right now!"

D.J. agreed. "If somebody was alone out here and stepped in that thing, he could die!"

Alfred glanced around fearfully. "Let's get out of here! There may be other traps!"

D.J. hesitated. "If we do that, we'll never find that white raccoon. Let me get these snares to take with us, then let's go on. But let's be mighty careful where we step."

Alfred sighed. "I should have known you'd say that! Whoops! Bugler's struck a trail!"

D.J. felt his blood quicken. From a distance Bugler began baying. Hunters said he was a "pappy hound," "strike dog," or had a "cold nose." That meant he could smell a scent long after the bear, mountain lion, bobcat, raccoon, or other game animal had passed.

But what made Bugler special was that he was a rare bawl-mouth hound.* That's what hunters called a hound with such an unusual baying cry that it stirred the emotions of anyone who has ever followed hounds on a frosty night.

D.J. listened a moment. "Sounds like it's a hot trail! Maybe it's the white raccoon! I'll turn Hero loose now!"

The scruffy mutt strained against his leash until D.J. freed him. Then Hero dashed off into the night trailing his sharp, chopping bark behind him.

Alfred asked, "If it *is* the white raccoon and they tree him, should we just mark the tree and come back with our box trap tomorrow night?"

"No sense dragging that trap around until we know about where to set it. Knowing the one tree from last night won't be enough to mark the ringtail's territory."

Alfred asked, "Want to run after them or sit here and wait until they've bayed whatever it is?"

"Let's sit and listen awhile. Tell me what you learned about raccoons from your encyclopedias."

The boys moved closer to the river where there was gravel and less brush. Hero's and Bugler's voices were echoing off the canyon walls. D.J. sat down on a big boulder that had been smoothed by countless years of spring snow runoffs feeding into Mad River.

Alfred scrunched down against another large boulder that protected him from the biting wind.

"One thing we forgot about, D.J."

"What's that?"

"If that mean man—Sky whatever his name is—is around here, he'll sure hear those dogs. He might come looking for us."

"It's a free country! We've got a right to be here. Now, tell me what you found out."

"Well, let's see. Raccoons are about three feet long, counting their tails. They're nocturnal and omnivorous."

D.J. nodded. "OK, 'coons come out mostly at night and they'll eat about anything. What else?"

"They're arboreal—live in trees—and, of course, they have the black mask around their eyes."

D.J. nodded, looking at the moon. It was casting shadows from a black oak tree's limbs. The wind had blown all the leaves down. The limbs made little shadows like bars across Alfred's face.

Something moved in the brush behind the boys. They spun around, flashing their lights. A tiny pair of eyes peered brightly at them. A small black animal with white stripes stood in the lights.

"Skunk," Alfred whispered.

D.J. whispered back. "Don't move! Just sit real still! It's OK unless he goes up on his front legs to warn us he might spray!"

"If he makes one move like that, I'm gone!"

The boys waited quietly, watching the skunk. He looked at them with small bright eyes for a moment but didn't seem alarmed. He waddled off, dragging his oily-looking tail. It left marks in the dust.

D.J. snapped his light off. "Is it true that raccoons always wash their food before they eat it?"

Alfred's light followed the skunk until its black and white fur was lost in the underbrush. He turned off his flashlight. Moonlight flooded the area again.

"Not really. That's kind of a legend. Oh, something else! Raccoons have very, very sensitive fingers, like hands. They can feel underwater for food and catch it without seeing it."

"Well, I wish we'd see that white one sitting on a big old tree branch with the moon behind it! Wouldn't that be a sight to see?"

Alfred agreed. "It would be nice, but I'm more interested in not seeing that Sky man we met last night. He won't like it when he finds out we let that deer go and took two of his snares."

"Listen!" D.J. said, stiffening his body.

Both boys sat motionless, hearing the gurgle of the river and the dogs working a hot trail.

Finally Alfred whispered, "What did you hear?"

D.J. shook his head and let out his breath. "Nothing, I guess." He lowered his chin into the collar of his coat to keep warm.

A sudden crashing sound made both boys swivel around and look up the mountainside away from the river. Something was smashing through the brush with such speed and power that it was crushing everything in its path.

"A bear!" Alfred cried, leaping to his feet. "Run, D.J.! **RUN!**"

Chapter Five

SECRET IN DEVIL'S SLIDE CANYON

D.J. jumped up and snapped on his light. He saw the underbrush waving violently. Small trees and dry limbs cracked sharply. But the earth rumbled so loudly the boy knew it wasn't an angry bear charging downhill.

Then his flashlight caught a movement below the thrashing brush. A big boulder was hurtling down upon him!

"Look out!" D.J. yelled. For a moment, he held his light on the frightening sight. Then he flipped the light down near his feet, looking for a way to escape. His beam showed another boulder beside him. Instantly, D.J. dove behind it though it was so close to the river he felt water hit his boots.

D.J. lost sight of Alfred. D.J. pressed against the smaller boulder and heard the bigger one rumbling faster and faster toward him. There was a horrible

grinding sound as the boulder struck D.J.'s smaller
one. He felt his boulder shudder. The runaway
wobbled unsteadily on top of the stationary one and
seemed to hang in midair for a second. Then the great
stone sailed over D.J.'s head and landed in the river
with a mighty splash.

After a moment, D.J. slowly raised his head and
shone his light on the water. The boulder was still
settling, sending up bubbles around it.

"Whew! That was close!" He flipped his light back
to the bank. "Alfred? Where are you?"

"Over here!" The voice was shaky and weak.

D.J.'s beam caught his best friend cautiously
peeking out from behind the wide stump of a Douglas
fir that had been cut down.

D.J. called, "You OK?"

"I-I think so. Just scared and scratched up some.
Wow! How do you suppose that thing broke loose?"

Alfred turned his light on the boulder. The water
was now rushing around it in white spray.

"No telling," D.J. replied. He tipped his light up
the hill the way the danger had come. "Boy! Look how
it smashed everything flat!"

"Just be glad it wasn't us!" Alfred said, his voice
still quivering from fright. "Hey! The dogs are barking
'treed'!"

"Let's go!" D.J. cried. "They're not far!"

The boys were glad to get away from the boulder
area and get over their fright. As they fought their way
through underbrush and under tall conifers, they
could hear Bugler's magnificent baying and Hero's
sharper, louder bark.

"You suppose it's the white raccoon?" Alfred

panted, ducking around a cedar tree.

"Sure would be nice!" D.J. stumbled and almost fell into his flashlight's beam. He recovered his balance and ran on.

The boys slid down an embankment, jumped fallen logs by the river's edge, and came at last to where they could see the dogs. A cottonwood tree with bright yellow leaves seemed to shimmer in the cold moonlight.

At the tree's base, Bugler was so anxious to get at the game in the twenty-foot tall cottonwood that he was biting off chunks of the bark. Hero was leaping high into the air and falling back in vain efforts to reach whatever was hidden in the rustling leaves up above.

Both boys aimed their flashlights toward the tree. For a moment, there was nothing visible. Then a pair of eyes glowed where a big limb left the trunk near the top.

"There!" A puff of white steam marked D.J.'s word as it exploded into the cold night air. "See it?"

"What is it?" Alfred asked, moving around so his light could penetrate the prey's hiding place.

D.J. saw a small animal about the size of a big tomcat suddenly stand up from where it had been crouching. "It's a bobcat! Look out! He's moving!"

The animal came down the tree trunk so fast it didn't seem to touch anything at all. Still well above the ground, it suddenly leaped into space.

"Watch out!" D.J.'s cry was almost too late.

The animal sailed across the face of the moon. It struck the ground running. The dogs were almost upon it, but the cat was amazingly quick. In two bounds it was away from the river. As the dogs barked furiously behind it, the bobcat sprang into another taller cottonwood.

D.J. breathed a sigh of relief, for the small, shorttailed cat is one of the most fearsome fighters in the wild. Both dogs could have been seriously hurt.

The boys tried to calm their dogs down while they played their lights on the treed animal. It hissed and spat at them from the safety of a high limb outlined against the moon.

"Sure wish that was the white raccoon!" Alfred said softly.

"Well," D.J. said at last, "we don't want this cat. Let's put the dogs' leashes on them and lead them away. Otherwise, they'll stay here bellowing all night."

"They're sure hurting my ears," Alfred admitted. He caught Bugler by the collar, but the excited hound kept trying to twist away and get at the treed cat. D.J. had the same problem with Hero.

Finally the boys dragged the protesting dogs away and back down the way they'd come.

D.J. said, "Maybe we'd better get home now so we'll get enough sleep to make it to Sunday School on time."

"Could we first take a look at where that boulder came from D.J.? See what caused it to break loose and almost kill us?"

The boys tied the dogs to a small ponderosa and scrambled up through the broken brush along the path the boulder had made. Their lights finally settled on the slight depression where the boulder had laid for years.

"Hey!" D.J. whispered, bending over and shining his light close to the ground. "Look at that!"

His friend knelt and moved his flashlight to shine on freshly-turned chunks of dirt.

"What'd you make of it, D.J.?"

"Looks like crowbar or pry bar marks. See?"

Alfred gently touched a foot-long rock near where the huge boulder had been dislodged. "This rock was used as a fulcrum!"

"A *what?*"

"You know! A support on which a lever turns in raising something! The bar was laid across this rock! See how the rock cracked from the weight as somebody leaned on the other end of the bar?"

D.J. whispered, "You mean it didn't just break loose by itself?"

Slowly, D.J. straightened as the meaning hit him. Then he rapidly flicked his light around the area and stopped the beam. "Look! A man's boot track! Come on, Alfred! Let's get out of here!"

Alfred didn't need any urging. Both boys scrambled back through the broken brush the boulder had taken. They untied the dogs and ran back toward the way they'd come.

Only when they'd reached the top of the canyon, panting hard and their muscles screaming for rest, did they stop.

The friends looked down into the darkness. Mad River was a thin thread far below. The moon was starting to sink on the western rim of the canyon. But the cold light still made a path across the river. The water looked like thousands of shiny silver dollars shimmering far below them.

"Alfred, that guy was watching us all the time,"
D.J. said tiredly, trying to catch his breath.

"You mean Sky?"

"Who else? If he had hit us with that boulder, it
would've looked like an accident! Nobody would have
known what really happened to us!"

His friend shivered. "He wasn't just trying to scare
us away this time!"

"He sure wasn't! That must mean he's hiding
something!"

"But what, D.J.?"

"Remember the kid—Cletus—said the man wasn't
really his father?"

"Yeah?"

D.J. took a deep breath. "It obviously has
something to do with that new kid we saw last night.
They've got some kind of secret."

"Well, they can *keep* it a secret for all I care, D.J.! I
don't want to solve any mystery bad enough to get
clobbered!"

D.J. nodded. He took a good grip on Hero's leash
and turned toward the county road that would lead
them home. "Funny thing about that kid. Somehow,
I think I've seen him someplace."

"Yeah? Where?"

"I don't know. But maybe it will come to me."

The boys hurried toward home. D.J.'s mind was
really churning out thoughts. They were all scary.

He said, "Alfred, even though the sheriff's office or
the game warden can now investigate because of the
poacher's snares, they may not believe that Sky tried
to kill us with that boulder."

"You mean that if we're going to keep after that

white raccoon, we're going to be in bigger danger than we are already?"

"If Sky's got a good enough reason, he might even come after us wherever we are."

Alfred stopped to catch his breath. "If you're trying to scare me, D.J., you're doing a mighty good job!"

D.J. didn't answer. He knew he and Alfred probably were in the greatest danger of their lives.

Chapter Six

THE PADDLE-FOOTED STRANGER

Sam Dillon's gruff voice seemed to rattle D.J.'s bedroom door. "Rise and shine! Time to get dressed for Sunday School!"

D.J. awoke with a start, then groaned and rolled over. "In a minute, Dad," he said sleepily.

"Breakfast in ten minutes!" Dad's voice was already fading down the hallway. A moment later, D.J. heard his father calling nine-year-old Priscilla to get up.

The boy lay in bed, staring at the ceiling. He didn't want to get up. Nothing had gone right lately. He'd been awake a long time last night, thinking about the poacher's snare and the boulder that could have killed him or Alfred.

What was Sky hiding that made him do such a thing? Was it worth the risk of hunting the white raccoon when Sky made it so dangerous?

49

And what about Grandpa moving out alone?

Troubles were piling up everywhere, and D.J. didn't know what to do.

Dad clumped back past D.J.'s door and banged heavily on it. "I don't hear you stirring, D.J.!"

"I'm up! I'm up!" D.J. called. He rolled slowly out of bed and pulled an old blue robe over his pajamas. Until Dad had remarried, D.J. had always slept in his underwear. But Two Mom had bought him a pair of pale green pajamas and insisted he wear them. Dad had enforced the rule.

D.J. opened the door just as his half-sister went scooting past him in the hallway. She cried, "I get the bathroom first!"

D.J. started to protest and race her, but she was by him and slamming the bathroom door before he could really get moving. He caught only a glimpse of her brown hair. It always seemed untidy, like an eagle's nest that had fallen on a fence post.

Feeling grumpy, the boy went on down the hallway and into the kitchen. He leaned against the door frame. His stepmother was preparing steel cut oats* in a pot.

"You were out late," she said, glancing at him.

"Not too late, Two Mom."

Dad sipped black coffee from an old mug he said he'd had since his Navy days. "How late were you?"

Sam Dillon was a powerfully-built man with a huge chest that seemed out of proportion to his short legs. His broad, stubby hands were calloused from his work as a choke-setter.* Dad was about the strongest man D.J. had ever seen. Dad's face was a deep sun-browned color. He had a thick neck and powerful shoulders.

The boy stifled a yawn. "I don't know. But I'm up and I'll be ready for Sunday School on time if Pris ever gets out of the bathroom. Where's Grandpa?"

Dad and Two Mom exchanged glances. D.J. sensed something, but didn't know quite what it was. Dad said casually, "Oh, he's out walking."

Two Mom turned down the flame under the pan and spoke directly to her husband. "We may as well tell him, Sam."

D.J. shoved himself away from the door frame. He approached the table and sat down opposite his father. The boy asked, "Tell me what?"

Dad wrapped his strong hands around the coffee cup. "Your grandfather has decided to move out and live by himself."

That wasn't news to D.J. But he didn't say anything.

Dad set his cup down on the table and looked directly at his son. "It's tough enough for two families to try to make one, as we are. Stepfamilies have to adjust to each other, as we discussed when I was thinking of marrying Hannah. But with three generations of mixed families, like ours, it's even harder to work things out. Your grandfather says he wants to be on his own."

D.J. remembered when he and Dad had talked about making one family out of two. For a long time, the boy hadn't like the idea. Pris was always a pain in the neck to him, and it wasn't easy having her as a stepsister. It wasn't easy having another woman replace his mother either.

After Dad's remarriage, D.J. looked up some

statistics on stepfamilies. About 1,500 stepfamilies with children under age 18 were formed daily. That was more than a half million "blended" families each year. Only a lot of them didn't blend very well. Experts said it took three to five years to work out the problems in a new stepfamily. But Two Mom always said, "This is a Christian family, and it'll work out."

D.J. said, "Grandpa told me he wanted to move out on his own. But where will he go?"

Dad answered. "Brother Paul knows the man who built that house where your grandfather, your mother, you, and I used to live. That man built another house exactly like it that is about to be moved or torn down."

Dad stopped and sipped his coffee. The boy frowned, not understanding.

Two Mom explained, "The man agreed to have the house moved instead of destroying it. He'll give it away if somebody will come haul it off in pieces or as it is."

D.J. had a sudden hope. "You mean there's a chance Grandpa. . . ?"

Dad nodded. "The house is his, and Brother Paul said he was sure that men from the church would help move it or put it up again."

D.J. asked thoughtfully, "Where are they going to put it?"

"On the same foundation where we used to live," Dad answered. "The landowner said he'd donate the space to have someone living on the property."

"Wow! That's great! I miss that old place!" the boy cried. "That was where I first started trying to write, where I got Hero, and my bear cub, and—"

He stopped. He didn't say it, but the words leaped into his mind. *And that's where my mother died.*

D.J. got up suddenly, crossed the kitchen in quick steps, and hurried down the hallway to pound on the bathroom door. "Pris! You going to stay in there all day?"

Dad's voice thundered. "D.J.!"

"She primps for hours!" the boy replied. "Then she'll make me late and you'll be mad at me!"

D.J. hurried into his own room and closed the door hard. In spite of Grandpa having a possible place to live, he'd still be alone. That wasn't good. And then there was the problem with Sky and the white raccoon. The bad feeling D.J.'d had on awakening seemed to get worse.

It stayed that way through Mrs. Stagg's teaching the Sunday School class at church. Alfred wasn't there, which surprised D.J. somewhat. He was really feeling glum when the church service started.

D.J. wanted to slip outside and be by himself, but Dad wouldn't allow it. So the boy sat in the very last row and felt all alone in spite of all the people around him.

The singing didn't help either. It was one of those mornings when the hymns seemed sad instead of bright and uplifting. D.J. couldn't quite understand why he was feeling so "down," but he found himself almost enjoying the feeling.

Brother Paul Stagg got up to preach. The rumble of his mighty voice coming up from his big chest seemed to make the little church shake.

"Please turn in your Bibles to First Thessalonians, chapter five, verse eighteen."

D.J. heard the rustle of many pages being turned. He didn't care. He let his mind roam free.

Why isn't Alfred here? He planned to come. If he were here, D.J. thought, *maybe we could talk things over and I wouldn't feel so glum.*

D.J.'s mind floated farther away from the sound of the preacher's voice. D.J. frowned. *Where had the man come from who had set the snares and loosened that boulder? Why would he do such a terrible thing? Certainly not because of a white raccoon! No, there had to be another reason.*

Brother Paul slapped his ham-size fist down on the homemade pulpit so hard that D.J. jumped. He caught the big man's words.

"Now notice two verses before that, Paul the Apostle tells us to 'rejoice evermore.' See it? Good! Now, in verse seventeen, he adds, 'Pray without ceasing.' And then the apostle tells us flat out, 'In everything give thanks; for this is the will of God in Christ Jesus concerning you.' "

There were some murmured "Amens" from what D.J. had heard called the 'amen corner' down front.

The boy shook his head. *How can I rejoice when somebody wants to kill me? How can I pray when Grandpa is moving out into the country all by himself? How can I give thanks for having a stepsister who aggravates me? How can I give thanks for anything this morning? That can't really be the will of God! Not with all the troubles I've got!*

D.J.'s mind came back to Alfred. He decided that right after the church service, he'd go find out about his friend.

Brother Paul was getting warmed up in the pulpit.

His reddish hair glinted as a ray of weak autumn sunlight poked through a place in the window where the paper "stained glass" had peeled back.

"When you count your troubles instead of your blessings," he cried, moving his big hands in a wide gesture, "you see earth's mud—and you miss God's stars."

D.J. slumped farther down in his seat. *Maybe so,"* he thought, *but right now it's daylight. I can't see any stars, but I can sure see lots of mud!*

When the Dillons got home from church, Grandpa was sitting in his old red rocker on the front porch. He smiled and waved his Irish shillelagh in greeting as Dad turned the family sedan into the driveway. Dad, Two Mom, and Pris went through the near side door into the house. D.J. walked around front.

"Hi, Grandpa. You missed church."

"Had to be done, D.J." The old man lifted his cane toward the street. "I was out in God's own natural church this morning, looking at the colors in the leaves and hearing the wind singing in the pines. Mighty restful and purty!"

The boy turned to follow the cane tip's sweep. "Sure is," he admitted.

Grandpa stopped rocking and leaned slightly forward. "You OK, D.J.?"

D.J. was quite concerned about Alfred, but since the Milfords didn't have a phone, D.J. would have to walk across town to his friend's house. He forced a smile.

"Sure—I'm fine."

Grandpa said, "I feel the need for another walk. How about coming with me?"

D.J. nodded. He opened the front door and called out to his father. Dad said to be back in half an hour for lunch. D.J. closed the door and walked beside Grandpa down the steps to the sidewalk.

They hesitated a moment and then turned uphill, away from Stoney Ridge. They walked in silence awhile, kicking the fallen leaves and watching more flutter down from the trees.

Grandpa asked, "Something troubling you, D.J.?"

Again, the boy shrugged. How could he explain a feeling that was heavy and thick, sitting on his shoulders like a living weight?

Grandpa gently flipped a bright red maple leaf over with the rubber tip of his cane. "Lookee there, D.J.! Ain't that about as purty a thing as ever a man could see?"

D.J. didn't feel like enjoying anything, but he nodded. He stared at the leaf without really seeing it.

Grandpa raised his cane. "Now, on the other hand, that there's one of the sorriest-looking dogs I ever did see."

D.J. raised his eyes. The animal was probably part pointer. He was about medium height, mostly white with some splotches of black. He had button ears, a roach back,* ewe neck, and a crank tail. It probably had been caught in a door sometime, for there was a sharp angle near the end where the tail had broken and healed without setting.

The chest was narrow and the ribs seemed trying to break through the short hair. But the most noticeable thing about the dog was his poor movement. He threw his front legs out to the side in what dog fanciers call "paddling."

Grandpa muttered, "I've seen more meat on a sackful of sticks! And look at him walk, would you? He's got a genu-wine paddle-footed gait that's enough to disgrace any dog!"

"No collar," D.J. said, ready to let the dog take the curb and pass. "A stray, probably. Somebody dumped him off."

Grandpa stopped and bent toward the skinny dog. "Howdy, Stranger." Grandpa's voice was gentle. Slowly, the old man extended the back of his left hand toward the animal. The dog's sad brown eyes suspiciously watched the cane in Grandpa's other hand.

He chuckled. "My Irish shillelagh bother you some, Stranger? Here, let me lay it down on the sidewalk. Now, nothing in either hand. See? Want to smell me and see I won't hurt you?"

The dog's eyes shifted to D.J. The boy wasn't impressed with the stray, but Hero wasn't exactly the world's handsomest dog either. D.J. also bent and slowly extended the back of his hand.

"Me too," the boy said. "See, Pooch? No harm intended from either of us. Now, how about you?"

Slowly, cautiously, the dog stretched his neck forward. He kept his feet well under him and tensed, ready to spring away.

"Scared, are ye, Stranger?" Grandpa asked softly. "Well, I guess you've seen your share of troubles in this world. But we're friends, my grandson and me. You want to be our friend?"

The dog responded to the gentle words. Very slowly the deformed tail moved in a friendly twitch.

Grandpa carefully touched the dog's lumpy head.

The animal cringed, but he didn't spring away.

"D.J., this here stray needs a home; that's plain as the nose on your face. I need a companion when I move out on my own again. I'm a'going to take this here dog with me!" Grandpa straightened up in firm decision.

D.J. shook his head. "Two Mom's allergic to dogs! She won't even let me take Hero inside the house."

"Hmm?" Grandpa petted the dog more. It responded slowly, beginning to trust. "It'd only be for a short spell. Anyway, I'll just have to work something out! The Bible says to be careful how you treat strangers because maybe they're 'angels unaware.'"

D.J. managed a smile. "Grandpa, that's talking about angels looking like *men*—or something like people anyway—not *dogs*."

The old man grinned. "Well, it don't make no never mind! Stranger here's going to know some hospitality, starting right now!"

"Stranger?"

"Sure! Dog's got to have a name, don't he? Come on, Stranger! Let's go home and see if you're welcome."

D.J. watched the old man turn toward the house, the paddle-footed mutt happily bouncing along beside him.

"Boy!" D.J. muttered, falling into step behind his grandfather and the dog, "there's one more trouble for me to count today!"

A DAYLIGHT WARNING

D.J. led the way to Hero's homemade doghouse in back of the Dillon home. The boy unsnapped his dog's chain from the collar and spoke firmly. "Hero, this is going to be Grandpa's dog, Stranger. You treat him nice, you hear?"

Hero and the stray dog wagged their tails and became instant friends.

Grandpa picked up Hero's chain and snapped it around the white dog's skinny neck. "I know Hero won't run away, but you might, Stranger, so I'll just use this little insurance on you until I see which way the wind's blowing with my new daughter-in-law."

Grandpa didn't say a thing about the stray dog all during lunch. D.J. was glad, because he already had enough problems for one day without being involved in another.

As Pris cleared the dishes and Two Mom poured

coffee for herself and the two men, D.J. saw a chance to get away.

"Dad, since Alfred didn't come to church, I'm going to check on him. OK?"

Two Mom asked, "Why don't you phone him?"

"He still doesn't have a phone, and I don't like to ask the lady who runs the little store to walk up those steps and call him down to answer."

Grandpa's pale blue eyes lit up. "Now, just a cotton-picking minute here, D.J.! You can't go off and leave me right now!"

Dad glanced at his father. "Why can't he?"

"Well. . . . " Grandpa hesitated, squirming a little. "I . . . well, I was kinda counting on D.J. to back me up."

"Back you up on what?" Dad demanded suspiciously.

D.J. stood up and excused himself. "Grandpa, I think you'd better just handle this on your own. 'Bye everyone! I'll be back for supper."

The boy grabbed his jacket and hurried across town toward Alfred's place. D.J. felt a little guilty about leaving Grandpa alone to talk Two Mom into letting him keep Stranger. But D.J. was more concerned about why Alfred hadn't shown up at Sunday School.

Alfred lived clear across town and out in the country on Lime Kiln Ditch Road. D.J. was used to walking, so he hurried down the hill toward town. The rising wind was driving fallen leaves down the deserted streets. Clouds were sliding in fast ahead of a storm. Everything gave D.J. a gloomy feeling.

He was almost through the small business section

of Stoney Ridge near the far edge of town. He was two steps past the local pool hall and bar when he heard the battered door squeak open behind him. The stench of stale beer and smelly cigarettes struck D.J.'s nostrils.

A man's voice hit him from behind. "Hey, you! Kid!"

D.J. didn't want to turn around, but his head spun as on a swivel. Durant Skiver, the mean man from Devil's Slide Canyon, stood there. He rolled a toothpick in the corner of his mouth and spoke.

"Yeah, I mean *you!*"

D.J. saw Sky was big. He wasn't as tall as Brother Paul, but Sky was still a big man. Even in the autumn briskness, he wore a dirty white T-shirt with short sleeves. His bare arms, heavily freckled, were as big around as telephone poles. The tops of his shoulders bulged with muscles. His chest seemed to D.J. to be as wide as a barn door. Blue jeans seemed to ride low on his hips. He spread his legs wide and set his dusty boots firmly.

"What's your name, Kid?"

The boy swallowed twice before answering. "D.J. Dillon."

"Well, D.J. Dillon, I've had enough of your trouble-making!" The man spoke softly and yet with a touch of controlled anger.

The boy licked his lips and glanced around. There wasn't another person in sight. "Trouble-making?" The word was almost a croaking sound because D.J.'s throat was so dry and tight.

"I *told* you to stay out of that canyon, didn't I?" Sky was upset. He flexed his biceps and hunched his shoulder muscles.

"I . . . it's government land, and not posted. . . . "

"I posted it!" The words were flat and hard, hitting like a blow. "But you decided to pay no mind to what I told you! Then you let a deer out of one of my booby traps, and stole them! Those snares cost money and take time to make!"

D.J. waved toward the edge of town. "I've got to go."

"You'll go when *I* say and *not* before!" Sky took a step forward, keeping his legs well braced.

"Look, mister, I—"

The man interrupted. "I'll teach you to put wild ideas into my son's head!" Sky took another step forward and reached out his powerful right forearm. D.J. instinctively drew back, but the hand clamped hard as a snapping turtle around the boy's wrist. Pain shot through his hand and arm.

D.J. protested, "I didn't put any ideas into anybody's head! I hardly spoke to that kid!"

"You must've said something!" Sky's hand squeezed tighter about the boy's wrist. "He's been acting peculiar the last couple of days! And you stop thinking about the white 'coon too! If Cletus is telling the truth, and there *is* such a critter, it's mine!"

"But. . . . " D.J. began, not wanting to show fear or be pushed around.

" 'But' nothing!" The man interrupted. Then he added softly, "You know something, D.J. Dillon? I don't like you even a little bit."

The bar door squeaked open again and D.J. saw the new kid, Cletus. It was against the law for anyone under age 21 to be in the bar, D.J. knew. But apparently Sky didn't care. D.J. saw Cletus' dark eyes widen as he hurried forward.

"Please, Pap! Don't hurt him!"

"Shut up, Cletus! Go wait in the pickup!"

"Please, Pap!"

"Move, I said!"

The kid almost ran to the rusty old pickup that once had probably been pale blue or green. D.J. glimpsed a gun rack across the truck's back window. He recognized a heavy rifle and double-barreled shotgun resting in the rack.

"Mister," D.J. began again, "you're hurting my wrist!"

Sky's lips curled up in something like a smile, but it had a hard, cruel look. "This is nothing compared to what will happen if I ever see you in that canyon again, or talking to my boy. And that goes for talking to anybody about me or Cletus—especially the law! You hear me?"

"I—yes—I hear you."

The painful grip loosened. "And tell your friend with the thick glasses the same thing! You hear?"

D.J. nodded and turned. He tried to not run, but he walked very fast toward Alfred's home. D.J. didn't even look back until he dropped, panting hard, on the bottom of the steps where Alfred lived.

When D.J. caught his breath, he climbed the steep stairs and knocked on the door. There was no answer.

D.J. frowned. "That's not like Alfred. Maybe his folks took him and his little brother for a drive to visit relatives out of town or something. Hm. What about the dogs?"

D.J. shuffled down the steps, pausing by the big

yew tree, feeling hurt and alone and scared. He glanced at the sky. Some very thin strands of clouds, almost like spun or cotton candy, were drifting in from the south. They blocked out the sun for a moment. A dark shadow fell across the whole area. D.J. shivered and ran around to the side of the house.

Neither Alfred's black and tan hound nor his little brother's dog, Dooger, were there. That didn't make sense to D.J. because Mr. Milford never took the dogs in the car with his family when they went visiting. Did that mean Alfred had gone hunting alone? D.J. shook his head. "No, he wouldn't go without me."

D.J. shoved his hands in his pockets and walked back around the house. The wind in the tall timber seemed to moan.

What was it Brother Paul preached about? "In all things give thanks"? A sudden gust of cold wind made D.J. hunch his shoulders deeper into his jacket.

He shook his head. *How can anybody give thanks at a time like this?* he thought. *Not one thing has gone right the last few days! There's no way God can expect me to believe that's His will!*

With his head down, D.J. walked in front of the little store that stood between the Milfords' rented house and the paved county road. Where was Alfred? If D.J. could just talk with his friend, maybe things would look better.

As he passed in front of the little store, the red door swung open so hard it hit D.J. on the left shoulder.

A gray-haired lady with half-glasses clutched a big grocery bag. "Whoops, I'm sorry! I couldn't see you! Are you hurt?"

D.J. barely glanced at the woman. "Naw," he said, brushing his shoulder. "It's OK."

"You sure?" She shifted the heavy bag. It had pictures of two kids and a heading: MISSING CHILDREN. There were some words under the photos.

"I'm sure." D.J. turned and went on into town. But at the edge of the small business district, he stopped. Sky's pickup was gone from in front of the bar, but the boy thought he might still be in town. D.J. tried to tell himself he wasn't really afraid, but there was no sense taking chances running into the man again.

D.J. turned sharply to his right and cut over to a side street.

He had only gone a few feet when a man's voice hailed him. "Hey, D.J.!"

Instinctively, the boy whirled, his heart leaping into his mouth. He hadn't heard the car pull up to the curb beside him.

"Oh, Brother Paul! Mrs. Stagg," he said with relief. He bent to look into the front seat where they were. Then he saw their daughter in the back. "Hi, Kathy."

The lay preacher had leaned across his wife's lap so he could talk through the open window. "Get in, D.J., and we'll give you a lift home."

The boy accepted immediately. He reached for the back door handle and slid in beside Kathy. She smiled and the whole car seemed to light up.

"Been over to Alfred's?" she asked, shoving a brown paper sack out of the way.

"Yes, but he's not home." D.J. suddenly wished Brother Paul was alone. It'd be OK to tell him about the new boy and his mean father—or whoever Sky was. But D.J. didn't feel comfortable talking about such things in front of Mrs. Stagg or Kathy.

"We ran out of milk," Mrs. Stagg said, turning in the seat. "We all decided to take a drive together and enjoy the autumn leaves before it storms. We picked up the milk on the way home. Can you stop by and have a cup of hot chocolate with us?"

D.J. hesitated. "Sure," he said. "Why not?"

All the way to the Staggs' home, D.J. tried to decide whether to tell Brother Paul about Sky and Cletus. D.J. hoped to have some time alone with the big lay pastor, but the Stagg family immediately went into the kitchen.

They made small talk as they seated D.J. at the table with Brother Paul. Kathy turned a stove burner on and set a small kettle over the blue flame. Her mother removed the milk carton from the bag. D.J. noticed pictures of two kids on the side of the milk carton. They weren't the same pictures he'd seen on the lady's grocery bag at the little store.

D.J. frowned as Mrs. Stagg opened the refrigerator door and put the milk inside.

Brother Paul's deep voice rumbled pleasantly. "What is it, D.J.?"

"I was just trying to think of something."

Kathy took the chair opposite him. "Think of what?"

"I don't really know. Something running around inside my head. Something I can't quite put my finger on! Something I'm trying to remember—"

Kathy teased, "Well, it's good to know *something*'s inside your head."

Mrs. Stagg gave her daughter a slightly disapproving look, but D.J. barely noticed. He leaped up from the table so suddenly he almost upset his chair.

"D.J.!" Mrs. Stagg exclaimed, startled. "What in the world . . . .?"

"Mind if I look in your refrigerator, please?" He didn't wait for an answer, but jerked the door open.

For a long moment he stared at the milk carton. Then he spun and threw out both hands in an excited gesture.

"That's it!" D.J. cried. "THAT'S IT!"

All three Staggs spoke at once. "What's it?"

D.J. exclaimed, "Now I know why—" He stopped abruptly, remembering Sky's warning.

Kathy urged, "Go on, D.J.! What do you know?"

Her father agreed. "Yes, tell us!"

D.J. again looked down at the milk carton. There was no doubt! But slowly he raised his eyes to meet those of the Staggs.

"I . . . I can't tell you," D.J. said softly.

Chapter Eight

WHERE IS ALFRED?

A few minutes later, his insides painful with the knowledge of what he'd just learned, D.J. was again on his way to Alfred's house. Brother Paul had volunteered to drive D.J.

He sat miserably in the front seat and stared unseeingly out the windshield. D.J.'s mind was whirling in desperation. *Should I tell Brother Paul anything? Sky had warned me to say nothing. But Alfred knows everything I do, except about the picture on the milk carton. It'd be OK to talk to him. But what about Brother Paul?*

The big lay preacher drove in silence. He seemed to sense his passenger's deep inner conflict. The boy closed his eyes a moment. His lips moved silently. "Lord, what should I do?"

He waited a moment, his eyes closed. The words from Brother Paul's sermon leaped into the boy's mind. *In all things give thanks.* That was crazy! D.J. shook his head, still not knowing what to do.

He felt the car slow. D.J. opened his eyes.

Brother Paul spoke for the first time. "Well now, D.J., I do believe that's your grandpa walking along the sidewalk. Is that dog with him?"

The boy glanced through the windshield. Grandpa Dillon was moving along with just a hint of a limp from his arthritic hip. The new dog was happily bouncing along beside him.

"Grandpa found him this morning," D.J. explained. "A stray. No collar or anything. Probably somebody dumped him off over by the highway. Skinny as an old horse."

Brother Paul asked, "Should we offer them a lift?"

D.J. shook his head. "Grandpa's just out for another walk, and I really do need to see Alfred."

"OK, D.J. Is your mother—uh—stepmother—going to allow Mr. Dillon to keep a dog? I mean, what with her being so allergic and all."

D.J. didn't answer. He didn't know. Ordinarily, he'd have stopped and found out because Grandpa had surely mentioned the idea to Two Mom. But D.J. was too anxious to see if Alfred was home yet.

As the sedan pulled up even with the old man, he turned around. D.J. saw Grandpa's grin start as he recognized Brother Paul's car.

They were passing Grandpa when he suddenly realized they weren't going to stop. He raised his Irish shillelagh and called out.

The driver touched his brakes. "Sorry, D.J., but if I don't stop, it'll be downright unneighborly of me, and your grandfather might not understand."

"But I've *got* to see Alfred!"

"I'll only be a minute! OK?"

The boy sighed. He could run on ahead, but he'd never get to Alfred's house before Brother Paul could say a few words to Grandpa and then drive on.

"OK," the boy replied softly. He rolled down the window on his side.

Grandpa came up and stuck his head inside the car. "Well now, howdy, Brother Paul! Giving my grandson a little ride to see the purty trees, are ye?"

"No, Caleb, I was just a'driving him over to his friend's house."

"Get out and see my new dog!" Grandpa spoke across D.J. to the driver. "Going to be with me when I move out on my own again!"

D.J. looked pleadingly at Brother Paul. He met the boy's eyes and nodded understandingly.

"Well, thanks right kindly, Caleb, but D.J.'s kind of in a hurry."

Grandpa waved the cane in the air. "Kids is always in a hurry! Won't hurt D.J. none to wait a minute whilst you look at my dog, Brother Paul. Ain't that right, D.J.?"

The boy couldn't explain and he couldn't expect his grandfather to understand if he didn't agree. He took a deep breath.

"Well, just a quick look, please."

Brother Paul dropped his hand on the boy's left shoulder. "I'll be quick as I can, D.J. You just sit still."

Grandpa was in one of his talkative moods, D.J. realized as the big lay preacher got out of the car and walked around to the curb. D.J. fretted, gazing out the windshield and trying to think about what he should do.

He closed his eyes, seeing the milk carton again. There were two pictures. He could see one of them really well in his mind. He hadn't taken time to read what was written on the panel under the pictures, but there was a phone number. An "800" number, D.J. remembered.

D.J. wasn't sure what he should do, except he had to talk to Alfred. The kids at school didn't call him 'The Brain' for nothing. Alfred was always full of bits of information about things. Besides, Alfred already knew about the mean man called Sky, the boy Cletus, and the white raccoon. So it'd be OK to talk to Alfred if he was home.

D.J. glanced at Grandpa. He was talking a mile a minute, gently tapping the stray dog with the tip of his cane and bragging on his fine points. Usually, D.J. would have smiled because that dog didn't really have one good thing anybody could say about him, except he liked Grandpa.

The boy cleared his throat. "Grandpa, I've got to get to Alfred's real fast. You've shown Brother Paul enough about that dog for now, haven't you?"

The old man's pale blue eyes opened in surprise. "Well now, D.J., you're sure a'rushing this visit with the preacher! And you ain't so much as asked me how your new stepmother took to me a'asking her about keeping this here dog until I can move into my own place."

"Grandpa, I just can't explain right now, but I absolutely have to get to Alfred's house!"

The old man started to protest, but Brother Paul interrupted quietly. "Now, Caleb, I'd be right proud to set a spell and talk dogs some more, but I plumb promised to get your grandson to his friend's house pronto. It's mighty important."

Grandpa didn't want to accept that, D.J. realized, but the big preacher grinned and said he'd come over later and finish the conversation. In a moment, Brother Paul was back under the steering wheel. He apologized and drove rapidly on through the main part of town toward the outskirts.

D.J. was so impatient to see Alfred that he sighed with relief when Brother Paul steered the sedan off the paved road. He eased onto the driveway leading past the little store to the Milfords' house.

The big man said, "Looks like we timed this just right, D.J.! Alfred's folks are just coming out of the store. See them?"

"Yes! Please stop here! Alfred's probably with them."

The big man automatically parked the car, cut the wheels against the curb, and set the hand brake. In the mountains, that was the only safe thing to do so cars wouldn't slip out of gear and roll down a hill. D.J. was out of the vehicle and running toward Mr. and Mrs. Milford before Brother Paul got his car door open.

Alfred's mother was a pleasant woman with sad brown eyes. Her mouse-colored hair was parted in the middle and tied back in a bun. She wore thick glasses like her son. She looked rather prim and proper, like an old-fashioned school teacher.

Her husband worked on the green chain gang* at the mill, but D.J. hardly noticed him as he rushed up.

"Alfred still inside?" D.J. called, motioning toward the little store.

John Milford looked surprised. "Why, no! Isn't he

with you?"

D.J. stopped short. "With *me?*"

"Yes," Mr. Milford replied, frowning and leaning down to look into the boy's eyes. "He left early this morning to meet you at Sunday School."

D.J. swallowed hard, hearing Brother Paul walking up behind him.

Mrs. Milford asked sharply, "You mean my Alfred didn't go to services with you today?"

D.J. turned to look up at the big preacher. He gently laid a ham-sized hand on the boy's shoulder.

"My wife said Alfred was absent from her Sunday School class."

Mrs. Milford's hands flew to her mouth. "Oh, no!" she whispered.

Her husband slipped his arm around her waist, but he looked straight at D.J.

"You haven't seen Alfred all day?"

D.J. shook his head and tried to swallow the scared feeling that was choking him. "No, I haven't. I came by awhile ago, but nobody was home."

Mr. Milford explained. "We drove our little son, Ralph, over to spend the day with his grandparents in Red Dog. Alfred had told us he'd probably go home with you for lunch and we'd pick him up later at your house, D.J."

Alfred's mother leaned forward and looked closely into D.J.'s eyes.

"You're not fooling me, are you, D.J.?"

When he shook his head, she turned to her husband. Her voice was almost a shriek.

"My Alfred's disappeared!"

Chapter Nine

RED LIGHTS AND SIRENS

In the next few minutes, D.J.'s mind whirled so fast his whole head ached. Everyone was asking questions except Mrs. Milford. She had let out such a shriek that Mrs. Greenlee, who owned the little store, rushed out. She led Alfred's mother up to her house behind the store.

John Milford's voice rose as he asked D.J. a lot of rapid-fire questions. Several people going into the store and coming out stopped to see what all the excitement was about. When Mr. Milford turned away from D.J. to talk to some of those people, the boy started to slip away to Brother Paul's car. The big lay pastor followed him.

D.J. turned around and looked up. "Please, Brother Paul! I'd like to be alone! I've got to think."

"Ordinarily, D.J., I'd leave you alone. But there's something you're not telling us! Does it have anything to do with Alfred being missing?"

D.J. hesitated, thinking fast. Finally he shook his head. "I don't see how it could. I just saw—" he hesitated.

He had almost blurted out that he'd seen Sky, the poacher, and he hadn't acted like a man who had just kidnapped somebody. But then, there was no doubt in D.J.'s mind about the picture he'd seen on the milk carton. That was the boy, Cletus. D.J. didn't know the exact difference between kidnapping and child stealing, but D.J. was certain Cletus was the missing child described on the milk carton.

But how could this have anything to do with Alfred disappearing?

Brother Paul opened the front door on the passenger's side of his car and let D.J. slide in. "Who'd you just see, D.J.?"

"I—can't say. Could you please take me home?"

"Mr. Milford will call the sheriff's office, and the deputy will want to ask you some questions, D.J."

"Please! I've got to get home to think!"

As the big man drove his sedan back onto the county road, he spoke in a gentle rumble. "D.J., I know you want to help your friend! So you're going to have to tell us what you're keeping back. We're going to need to know so we can find Alfred."

"I've told you all I can!" D.J. cried, covering his face with his hands.

As the car turned toward downtown Stoney Ridge, D.J. bent forward. He put both hands to his forehead.

He told himself, "Alfred isn't the type who'd just wander off. And he wouldn't lie to his folks and say he was going to meet me at church unless that's what he planned to do. Something must have happened before he got to church. But what?"

The boy raised his head and looked through the windshield, but his eyes didn't focus on anything. His mind was spinning faster and faster.

"I know Alfred wouldn't go off hunting without me," D.J. thought. "But why didn't he make it to church? And where are the dogs?"

There was no answer. The boy shook his head hard to clear his mind. "Maybe Alfred's not really missing! But if he is—if he's been kidnapped—then there's only one person who would've done that!"

D.J. remembered the conversation with Sky in front of the saloon. The kid called Cletus had come to D.J.'s defense even though the kid must have known he was likely to get "whupped," as he called it.

D.J.'s mind skipped to the milk carton. He'd first seen Cletus' picture on the carton when D.J. was preparing his cereal while talking to Two Mom. But he hadn't really noticed. Then, at the Staggs' house, he recognized the kid.

Cletus was the same boy whose picture was on the milk carton. Of course, the picture was at least five years old. The kid's hair was longer now, and he was taller. But D.J. had no doubt it was the same boy. Besides, hadn't Cletus blurted out that night at the river that the mean man wasn't really his father? And didn't the man keep the kid out of school? Of course, Cletus could have gone to another school even though he seemed to live within the Stoney Ridge school district.

"But," D.J. told himself, still staring unseeing out the windshield, "when that man talked to me a little while ago, he didn't act nervous. He didn't act as if he'd done anything. In fact, he warned me to tell Alfred to keep quiet too! Yet on the other hand, I know Sky has the missing kid pictured on the milk carton!

"So that guy's either a kidnapper or a child stealer. I don't know which is which, except it's against the law! And he threatened me and Alfred if we told about the white raccoon! What would he do if I told about the missing boy? And what's that got to do with Alfred disappearing?"

D.J. muttered aloud, "It just doesn't make sense!"

"What doesn't make sense?" Brother Paul's deep bass voice filled the car.

D.J. hesitated, wanting to share his terrible secret and yet being afraid. "Uh—well—Alfred disappearing."

"Can you tell me about it now?"

Again, D.J. hesitated, thinking fast. The mean man had warned him to stay away from Cletus. The man had warned Alfred and D.J. to stay away from the river where the white raccoon was supposed to have been seen. The man had threatened D.J. if he told the law about the nooses.

The runaway boulder last night proved the man was capable of really hurting someone. But if the man had kidnapped Alfred, then they would have been long gone from Stoney Ridge. Or the pickup would have been packed for traveling. But it was empty, because D.J. remembered the gun rack visible through the cab's rear window.

"I'm sorry, Brother Paul. I just can't!" D.J.'s eyes focused on the street ahead. He pointed. "Oh, there's Grandpa and his dog! Could you give them a lift?"

"Sure thing, D.J.! Let's hope that new dog of his is used to riding in a car!"

A moment later, the old man said, "Much obliged, Brother Paul." He closed the back door and laid his cane on the seat. Stranger lay on the floorboard, his bumpy head on Grandpa Dillon's feet. He put his left hand gently on the dog's head and spoke reassuringly for a moment.

"Glad we came along," the big man rumbled.

D.J. didn't say anything. His mind was back on Alfred's disappearance.

Grandpa Dillon spoke again. "Thanks kindly, Brother Paul! I was a'getting a mite tuckered! That there cold wind's cutting right to the bone! Going to come a corker of a storm, you can be sure of that! 'Course, I don't mind none, but Stranger here was a'shivering so hard he was about to shake his ribs loose from his backbone. Me'n Stranger was out thinking over what my new daughter-in-law said about keeping this here dog."

Ordinarily, D.J. would have asked what Two Mom had said. But Grandpa's words didn't really register on D.J.'s mind. He turned to look over the top of the backseat. "Grandpa, something's happened to Alfred."

The old man grunted and adjusted his bifocals with an age-spotted right hand. His other hand absently petted the dog.

"Now how in the world can anything happen to him that fast?"

"That fast?" Brother Paul asked, looking sharply in the rearview mirror at his backseat passenger.

"Yeah!" D.J. echoed. "What'd you mean?"

"Well, what'd you suppose I mean? I saw him a spell back whilst Stranger and me was a'walking."

"You saw Alfred?" D.J. cried, jumping up on the front seat with his knees. He peered over the back of the seat. "Where? Was he alone?"

"Well, yeah, he were a'foot and alone. But where was that? I don't rightly recollect. I was just moseying along, not paying no special attention, and we didn't get close enough to say howdy, but. . . ."

"Grandpa! Please! It's very important! When did you see Alfred? This afternoon?"

"Well, now let me see. Hmm? Could'a been this morning, or could'a been this afternoon."

"Grandpa!" D.J.'s word was filled with anxious pleading.

"Oh, now I recollect! It was right before you two stopped to talk to me awhile back."

D.J. and Brother Paul exchanged glances. The big man's eyes rolled up briefly and D.J. thought he could read the big man's lips. "Thank you, Jesus!"

"Think, Grandpa! You're sure he was alone?"

"Plumb by his lonesome!"

"No dogs?"

Grandpa shook his head. "I done told you! He was all by hisself!"

D.J.'s excitement was making the questions bubble out of him like soda pop on a hot day. "Where did you see Alfred?"

"Well, me'n Stranger was just a'passing that park, I think it was. Right about where the old cannon stands, you know?"

D.J. turned to speak to Brother Paul but the big man's huge hands were already turning the wheel. The tires squealed slightly as the sedan made a U-turn at the intersection and speeded back toward the park.

The boy took a deep breath and rocked on his knees. He grinned. "Grandpa, you don't know what a load you took off of my mind!"

D.J. turned around to watch as they approached the park. Most of the leaves had fallen and the trees were bare. It only took a glance to see that there wasn't anybody in the block-square park. D.J.'s heart sank.

Grandpa mused, "Don't see him now. But he was right over there by that cannon."

D.J. slumped into the seat, his hopes dumped again. He asked aloud, "Where could he be? Why didn't he meet me at church? And where are the dogs?"

The big lay pastor glanced at the boy. "We'll find him, D.J. But maybe it'd help if you told us why you got so upset when you looked at that milk carton this morning."

Grandpa leaned forward. "What's this about a milk carton?"

D.J. didn't answer. Brother Paul waited a moment and then said softly, "I saw what was on that carton. Couple pictures. Lots of different pictures on the cartons that come out each week. D.J., did you see one of those missing kids around here?"

The boy hesitated. He didn't want to lie, but he didn't want to say what he knew either. As he debated what to do, a siren sounded behind him.

"Oh! Oh!" Brother Paul said softly, glancing in the side mirror. "Here comes the sheriff's car! Guess he saw me make that U-turn back there. But I didn't

think it was illegal to do that!" He eased up on the
gas and turned toward the curb.

Grandpa turned to look through the rear window.
"Got his red light on and that there sireen just a'wound
up plumb tight! Brother Paul, you must'a done
something worst than make a U-turn."

D.J. didn't say anything. He knew even before the
sedan stopped against the curb that the deputy wasn't
after Brother Paul. It was bad news about Alfred!

The uniformed deputy jumped out of his patrol
unit car and ran around to D.J.'s side. He recognized
the officer as Corporal Arlis Brackett.

The deputy quickly opened the passenger side
door. "D.J., come with me! Hurry!"

Grandpa and Brother Paul protested, but the
deputy took the boy's arm and helped him out of the
car.

"There's no time to explain! Follow me back to the
Milfords' house if you want, but I've go to roll on a
Code Three!* Come on, D.J.! Let's move!"

In seconds, the patrol unit was roaring out of
town with its red light flashing and its siren wailing.

D.J. swallowed hard and managed to ask, "Did
you find Alfred?"

The deputy didn't take his eyes off the roadway.
"No, but we found something else!"

Chapter Ten

A CLUE TO ALFRED'S DISAPPEARANCE

Corporal Brackett parked his patrol unit up behind
the little store and turned off the siren. He ran around
the front end of the patrol unit and jerked D.J.'s door
open. "Upstairs! Fast!"

The boy followed the uniformed officer up the
steep stairs to the Milfords' front room. Alfred's parents
were waiting there. They began excitedly asking D.J.
so many fast questions his ears ached. The deputy
motioned toward one of the two big green chairs.
D.J. sat down, not understanding. The deputy turned
to Alfred's father.

"Where's the note?"

Mr. Milford reached inside his shirt pocket and
handed a piece of paper to the officer. He nodded and
turned to D.J.

"Read it, D.J." The note was shoved into the boy's
unsteady hand. The deputy spoke to Mrs. Milford.

"Where's the milk carton?"

D.J. had started to unfold the piece of paper, but he stopped and looked up in surprise. "Milk carton?" he asked.

"*Read!*" the deputy said firmly. "Mrs. Milford, could I have the carton, please?"

She turned back to the kitchen. D.J. forced his eyes down to the note. He recognized his best friend's neat handwriting.

> *Dear D.J.,* the note began.
> *I am leaving this note for you at my house since I could not find you. I started for church when I saw that man. He was alone. Then I remembered something I'd seen at breakfast so I came home and checked. I was right. My mom will show you the milk carton and you will understand.*
> *I have decided to help Cletus, so have taken the dogs. Wish you were with me.*
> *Your friend, Alfred.*
> *P.S. If I have any trouble, you will know where to look.*

Mrs. Milford returned from the kitchen with a carton of milk. D.J. instantly recognized the picture on the side panel.

Grandpa Dillon puffed through the front door, limping slightly and leaning on his cane. He didn't have Stranger. Brother Paul followed the old man into the house. The pastor removed his cowboy hat and ducked his head so he wouldn't hit the top of the doorjamb.

"Say!" Paul Stagg rumbled, walking up to take a closer look at the milk carton. "That's the same picture that shook you up at my house, D.J.!"

Alfred's father demanded, "What's going on here? Somebody had better tell me, and be quick about it!"

The deputy held up both hands, palms outward. His voice was calm and firm.

"Now, folks, I can understand how you're all rightfully worked up. But I'll ask the questions, if you don't mind. So why don't all of you take a seat and let me handle this my way?"

Reluctantly, Alfred's folks sat down on the sofa, their arms around each other for comfort. Grandpa took the other big green chair. Brother Paul eased into an old wooden rocker. He crossed his legs and tossed his hat over the toe of his cowboy boot.

The deputy stood facing the boy. "D.J., you wouldn't say anything on the way over here. Now I think you'd better tell us everything—and fast!"

Reluctantly, the boy did. An hour later, he was at home, dressing warmly to go help the officers rescue Alfred and Cletus—if they could beat the incoming storm.

D.J. felt miserable. He also felt better. The terrible burden of keeping a secret was gone. But the fear of what might have happened to Alfred was still a heavy weight on D.J.'s mind.

D.J. dressed quickly, aware the day was fast slipping away. He prayed silently, thinking how troubles kept piling up. Brother Paul's sermon flashed through the boy's mind again. "In all things give thanks."

D.J. shook his head. "How can anyone give thanks when things keep getting worse? If anything happens to Alfred. . . ."

His thoughts were interrupted by the sound of voices down the hallway. Through his closed bedroom door, D.J. could hear the deputy still trying to reassure Sam Dillon, Priscilla, and Two Mom. D.J.'s stepmother spoke loudly.

"I don't want him to go!"

Dad said firmly, "He's got to go so he can show the officers where he and Alfred saw the Cletus boy and his kidnapper that night!"

D.J. heard Corporal Brackett's answer. "That's right! We've called in one of our deputies who's also a dog handler. If the dog can pick up Alfred's trail, we should be able to find him before the storm breaks. Hopefully, we'll rescue that other boy too."

Two Mom's voice rushed on, clearly audible to the boy. "The TV weatherman says that storm's coming down out of the Gulf of Alaska! Could be the earliest snow we've ever had—and the worst for so early in the year! I don't want D.J. out in that weather!"

The deputy's voice was calm. "I can understand your concern, Mrs. Dillon. But look at it from the Milfords' viewpoint too. If their boy hasn't been stolen like that other kid—Cletus—then Alfred's likely to be caught in that storm unless we can find him fast. Mrs. Milford says Alfred's heaviest clothes are still in his closet. Guess he didn't know this storm was coming."

Two Mom's voice was almost shrill. "But surely you can't go down in that canyon at night! It's too dangerous, even without that terrible man down there with traps that could kill a person!"

"Our department is used to working at night, Mrs. Dillon. We're all experienced in wilderness survival."

Two Mom apparently wasn't listening. D.J. heard
her voice break. "And stealing children! What's the
world coming to, anyway?"

"Thousands of children disappear every year,
Mrs. Dillon. If we're lucky, we'll recover one of those
kids tonight. Hopefully, we'll also find Alfred. And
when we catch this man, he won't steal any more
kids!"

D.J. laced his heavy leather boots and heard his
father's voice down the hallway. "But if you fail, Arlis,
then Alfred will also be among those thousands of
missing kids. Right?"

The officer's reply was so low D.J. didn't hear. The
boy stood up and hurried down the hallway. He wore
full length thermal underwear under his heaviest
pants and wool shirt. He also had on fleece-lined
gloves, thick boot socks, a quilted parka, and an all-
wool stocking cap. He carried his five-cell flashlight.

His half sister ran toward him. She hugged D.J.
around the waist. "Don't go!" she pleaded. "Don't go!"

He spoke gently, patting her on top of her untidy
nest of hair. "I've got to! Alfred would do the same for
me."

The deputy said, "Let's roll, D.J."

"I'll get my dog."

"Sorry, but Hero might mess up the scent our dog
will try to follow. You'll have to leave Hero at home."

D.J. was disappointed, but he understood.

* * * * *

Two hours after dark, D.J. led Brother Paul and
four uniformed deputies with one scent dog down the
steep trail to the bottom of Devil's Slide Canyon.
Silently, they moved along a deer trail beside Mad

River. Finally D.J. stopped. He flashed his light's beam into the river.

"That's the boulder that almost hit us," he said, holding the beam steady so the men could see. "Over there's the tree where the kid said he saw the white raccoon." D.J. moved the light.

Except for that thin streak, the whole area was black as the inside of a whale. The cold wind had died at sunset. But before darkness, D.J. had seen gray snow clouds slipping quietly across the western rim of the canyon. It was deadly quiet. That's the way it usually got just before snow started falling.

Other flashlights flickered in the darkness beside the river. D.J. could see shadowy outlines of the men who were to conduct the search. Besides Brother Paul, there were two backup deputies whose names D.J. hadn't caught, and Deputy Hank Hubble. He was also one of Timbergold County's three dog handlers. D.J. had met Deputy Hubble and his Rottweiler scent dog during some experiences with the "mad dog" of Lobo Mountain.

Deputy Hubble seemed quite young, but he had the build of a weight lifter. His belt had a radio handset and a service revolver. Survival equipment was packed on his back. He had his dog, Razzmatazz, or Razz, on a stout leather leash.

In the flashlights' beams, D.J. saw the dog had a broad head and deep brown eyes. Razz was about two feet high at the shoulders. He was powerfully built with short, coarse black hair. He had tan markings on his chest, muzzle, cheek and over both eyes. His tail was docked close to his body.

The dog handler bent and unsnapped the leash.

He spoke softly to the dog. "OK, Razz, get to work!"

The dog first sniffed D.J.'s pants leg, then Brother Paul's. The Rottweiler moved on to smell the two backup deputies and finally Corporal Brackett. D.J. remembered that this was because the dog knew he was to find someone who wasn't present. In this case, that person was Alfred.

Corporal Brackett spoke. "No smell of wood smoke, so the cabin may not be close by. Or it may be that there's just not enough breeze to carry the smell this way. OK, Dan, I guess you'd better see what your dog can do."

By the flashlight's beam, D.J. saw Deputy Hubble reach into his coat pocket. He pulled out an undershirt. The dog handler explained.

"Mrs. Milford says her son changed out of this when he showered this morning. Here, Razz, get a whiff of this and let's find that kid."

A moment after smelling the garment, the dog turned and began thrashing back and forth through the brush, looking for a scent to match the undergarment. D.J. held his breath, hoping that Alfred had come this way.

Razz gave a low "whoof!" His stub tail rotated fast.

Deputy Hubble whispered, "He's got the scent! Come on, everybody! Quietly!"

Corporal Brackett warned, "Remember to watch out for snares!"

D.J. followed the dog and the men. He glanced anxiously at the sky. It had so perfectly blended with the top of the canyon that there was nothing visible except a deep darkness. The boy shivered just as something wet touched his cheek.

He automatically reached up and brushed it off with the tip of his right glove. He turned his flashlight on it.

"Snowflake!" he breathed. It was big and wet.

Razz turned abruptly away from the deer trail. His handler spoke softly.

"Razz is going into the brush. That means Alfred left the trail. We'd better find him fast! If it snows very much, the dog will lose the scent and we'll be wasting our time to go on."

D.J. groaned softly. His eyes rolled upward to the gloomy sky. "Oh, please! Not now! Haven't we got enough problems without the snow?"

Another big wet flake settled on the boy's eyebrows. He brushed it away. Another fell. D.J.'s light flickered upward. Dozens of huge flakes, a good inch across, were falling rapidly through the beam.

Suddenly, the dog handler stopped and whispered, "Lights off, everybody! I smell smoke!"

Total blackness engulfed the group as the lights were snapped off. D.J. could hear the men sniffing the still night air.

Corporal Brackett whispered. "I smell it too! Has to be from a fireplace or stove! That means the cabin must be close by. D.J., you stay here in case there's any trouble. We'll go on ahead and see if we can take the suspect without incident."

The boy started to protest, but the dog handler suddenly slipped and fell. D.J. heard him whisper, "I tripped over something. Let me check."

D.J. saw a thin pencil beam of light as Deputy

Hubble held his gloved hand across the lens. By opening his fingers a little, the officer controlled the light. D.J. caught a bit of reflected light in the brush.

"Trip wire!" The dog handler whispered excitedly. "Used to have them in 'Nam!"*

D.J. whispered to Corporal Brackett. "What's that mean?"

The deputy was tense, looking around in the darkness and straining to hear. After a moment, he answered the boy.

"It's a kind of homemade alarm. A wire hidden in the brush accidentally got kicked. The other end of the wire is probably tied to tin cans or something that rattled in the man's cabin."

D.J. could barely swallow. "You mean he probably heard us and knows we're here?"

"Yes, he might. Or he might think a deer or bear stumbled over his trip wire. We'll try to follow it to the cabin. You stay quiet!"

D.J. whispered hoarsely, "Brother Paul—you going to stay with me?"

"They might need me at the cabin."

"But—"

"You'll be OK, D.J." The big man's voice rumbled into silence. Brother Paul turned to follow the deputies and the dog into the darkness.

A moment later, D.J. was alone. He had never seen such darkness! D.J.'s lips moved. "Lord, I'm scared!"

Brother Paul's words from the sermon seemed to answer. "In everything give thanks."

The boy shook his head. "How can I do that? Everything's getting worse!"

The officers had been gone about five minutes when a slight sound from behind made D.J. swivel his head. He saw the glow of a flashlight with a hand across the lens. A thin streak of light released between fingers hit D.J. right in the eyes.

For a second, the boy thought it was one of the deputies. But it wasn't a friendly voice that growled angrily out of the night.

"So you *told*, did you? And you brought the *law!* Well, that's the *last* time you're *ever* going to do anything like that!"

D.J. felt powerful hands grab his shoulders. The boy instinctively twisted sideways and rolled. His flashlight was knocked from his hand and lost in the darkness.

D.J. leaped up. Desperately, he ran downhill through the brush straight toward the river—with the man chasing after him!

Chapter Eleven

A DESPERATE STRUGGLE

D.J. heard an angry whisper behind him. "Won't do no good, kid!" Sky removed his fingers from the flashlight so the full beam hit D.J.'s back. "I'll outrun you in five seconds—and then you're going to pay!"

The light created a huge shadow of the slender boy desperately plunging down the mountainside chased by a man with outstretched arms. The heavy clumping sound of Sky's boots behind him made D.J. run all the harder.

But as he raced under a giant ponderosa, D.J.'s boots slid on a carpet of slippery pine needles. His legs shot out from under him. He fell hard on his back. Flecks of bright light and little shooting stars exploded in his head. D.J. tried to leap up, but the flashlight bored into his eyes, blinding him.

"Gotcha!" Sky's powerful right hand plunged viciously through the light's beam for the boy's throat.

D.J. didn't think—he just reacted. Desperately he threw up his right arm. It hit the flashlight. It sailed up into the air, twisting around rapidly. The trees seemed to leap to life. They appeared to move in all directions as if fleeing from the scene.

Then the light turned earthward. It twisted down, making more fearful, leaping shadows. The light hit hard, lens down. D.J. heard the sound of breaking glass. The light went out.

Instantly, total darkness smothered D.J. But he could feel the man's hands trying to grab him. D.J. heard Sky's heavy breathing.

Again, without thinking, D.J. acted. He rolled sideways, ignoring the sharp pine needles and the short needle points of a pine cone. He rolled onto his hands and knees and leaped to his feet.

A powerful hand groped in the blackness. Through his stocking cap, D.J. felt strong fingers closing down hard. He ducked his head and jumped away. The cap slid off. Cold air struck his scalp like a razor. But D.J. didn't care. He bent low and ran hard into the thick darkness.

"Help!" D.J.'s call pierced the night and echoed off the sides of Devil's Slide Canyon. But there was no answering shout. There was only the puffing of an angry man behind him.

D.J. smashed into a low-hanging branch. He felt long pine needles scrape his cheek. Instinctively, the boy jerked his head away. He twisted sharply to the left and fell over a downed limb. He sailed through the blackness, throwing up his hands to protect his head against hitting a tree trunk.

But he landed in a shallow ravine. It was still

moist from recent frost and rain runoffs so the muddy bottom was slick as a frozen mountain pond.

"Ohhhh!" D.J. yelled as his feet shot out from under him. He slid down the ravine faster than a toboggan on packed snow.

Frantically, D.J. reached into the night to grab something to stop his mad ride. His gloved fingers touched small shrubs or tree limbs, but they were gone before D.J. could close his hands.

Faster and faster he flashed down the slick ravine. His legs smashed into invisible obstacles that twisted the boy's body but didn't slow him down. He felt his pants snag on sticks, stones, and tree roots. But nothing stopped his mad slide.

Then he heard something else ahead. A waterfall! Terror ripped a strangled cry from his mouth. "Oh, no!"

D.J. was sliding straight toward Mad River! He recognized the sound of Rainbow Falls. In an instant, the boy realized he was in one of the ravines that fed the pools. He had often fished for rainbow trout there.

It was a twenty-foot waterfall, but there were huge boulders just below the falls. Those boulders could break a boy's back or crunch his head like an eggshell.

"Oh, Lord! No!" The desperate prayer escaped the boy's lips as he grabbed frantically into the night.

But his heavy right boot hit something so hard his whole body was jerked violently aside. His right foot stayed where it was while his other leg and his body were thrust viciously into the night air. He realized instantly his foot was caught in a tree trunk.

But before D.J. could do more than throw up his

hands to protect his face, the right side of his head hit something a glancing blow. His right ear felt as though it had been torn off by the rough bark of a tree trunk.

Then the whole world seemed to explode into shooting stars and D.J. lay still in the night.

He opened his eyes to feel something wet and cold on his face. Still stunned, he brushed at the wetness with his gloved right hand.

Snow was falling so thick and fast that the whiteness made little pinpoints of light in the darkness.

Where am I? What happened? The thought took a moment to answer. The pain in his right ear brought back the memory. He gently touched the ear with his gloved hand. It hurt. Probably was bleeding too. But it wasn't fatal. D.J. knew the most important thing was to get away. He started to stand, but he sank back with a moan.

"Oh! My foot!"

Gingerly, reaching through the blackness, ignoring the fast-falling snow on his face, D.J. felt his right foot. It was wedged between two tree roots. Carefully but quickly, the boy's fingers searched for a way to free his foot.

A nearby branch moved softly in the darkness. It couldn't be the wind; there was none. There was only the strange stillness that came with an early snowfall. D.J. froze, gloved hands resting on the boot. His ears strained to hear.

At first, he heard only the rushing of the little waterfall as it plunged into the river. The nearby brush had quit moving as though someone or something was also stopped dead still, listening.

Then D.J. caught a faint noise of breathing! It was so close the boy felt he could have reached into the blackness and touched the big chest from where the heavy sound came.

Instantly, D.J. held his breath. He didn't even take a breath, but just stopped breathing. He wished he could still his pounding heart which thumped in his ears.

"Wuf!"

D.J. had heard startled wild bears before. This bear was within a few feet in the darkness. D.J. opened his mouth to yell; partly from fright and partly to scare the bear away.

But the bear "whuffed" again and spun away into the darkness. It smashed noisily through the brush away from the ravine.

Sky's voice came from close behind D.J. "Nice try, kid! But you can't fool me with that trick! I'll get you yet!"

D.J.'s pursuer rushed forward in the fast-falling snow. Sky took a startled breath when there suddenly was no ground under his feet. D.J. heard the man's body land solidly in the ravine where D.J. had just been.

There was a terrible shriek as the man's feet flew from under him. "Whoaaa!"

Sky hurtled by D.J. and down the last few feet of the ravine. D.J. couldn't see a thing, but he knew from the sounds when the man was near the top of the waterfall.

"Noooo!" The cry from the ravine's end told D.J. the man was airborne in the night.

A second later there was a big splash.

The boy strained to hear more, but there was only the sound of the river as it returned to its normal whirling and plunging.

For a long moment, D.J. hesitated. Now was his chance! He could finish freeing his foot and run. He could run back to the deputies and Brother Paul.

A desperate cry split the night; a sputtering gasp from the deep pool of Rainbow Falls.

"HELP!"

It came only once, then the swirling waters drowned out everything.

D.J. hestitated and wondered, *What should I do?*

Suddenly, someone on the riverbank below D.J. and to his left snapped on a flashlight. The beam probed toward the pool below the falls. D.J. couldn't see who held the flashlight. Neither could he see the pool. But he clearly saw in the flashlight's beam that the air was filled with huge, fast-falling snowflakes. From the way they sank straight down, D.J. knew they were heavy with water.

The boy finally jerked his foot free of the tree's limb and carefully stood up. His ankle hurt, but it wasn't broken. It would be OK, like his ear. D.J. glanced toward the river.

For the first time, he could see the bottom of the falls in the flashlight's beam. Sky was being tossed about in the foaming water like a cork on a stormy sea. Violent swirls of blue-green water dashed themselves into white foam against the partly submerged boulders. A big whirlpool sucked Sky under.

D.J. made up his mind. *I've got to help him!*

D.J.'s eyes turned down to try seeing some way

down from the little cliff top where he stood. He
started running, but his foot hurt. He slowed to a
hobble, moving away from the ravine so he wouldn't
fall in again. He picked his way toward the river,
helped by the faint glow of the flashlight reflecting
off the trees.

D.J. stopped a few feet back from the top of the
cliff top. He leaned forward and glanced below, trying
to find a way down the steep granite side to help
save the drowning man.

But there was no way except to jump into the
river, and that meant D.J. would be in the same
terrible spot as the drowning man.

Desperately, D.J.'s eyes went to the flashlight. Only
one light; one person! But *who?* One of the deputies?
Brother Paul?

"Alfred?"

D.J. breathed the name aloud. Then he cupped his
hands over his mouth and yelled. "ALFRED!" But his
friend couldn't hear above the roar of the waterfall.

Alfred was moving up toward the pool, obviously
trying to help Sky.

D.J. glanced down to his feet. Too steep! He'd
break a bone trying to go down that way. D.J. looked
upstream. That was worse! He gazed downstream.
That was the only way!

D.J. started feeling his way along the cliff
overlooking the river. He caught another glimpse of his
friend below.

Alfred's light showed Sky whirling in the water.
D.J. saw the beam flicker from place to place on the
ground. Then Alfred reached out and picked up a
long broken limb. Alfred's light flipped back to the

churning white water under the waterfall.

D.J. saw the limb lowered toward Sky. He grabbed for it. Alfred was almost jerked into the river as Sky desperately hung on.

D.J. cupped his hands around his mouth. "Hang on, Alfred! I'm coming! Don't fall in!" The roar of the raging river smothered his words.

D.J. had to watch where he was going, so he lost sight of his friend and the rescue effort below. It seemed to take D.J. forever to pick his way down from the waterfall's beginning to a deer trail in the riverbank. The flashlight's reflected beam didn't help here, D.J. realized. He sat down fast and scooted down the small deer trail.

Then D.J. was on his feet beside the river. He hobbled toward the flashlight's beam. D.J. felt the stones under his feet. He heard the roar of the water from the falls. But he couldn't see Alfred or hear him. D.J. couldn't see Sky either. Only the flashlight was in sight.

D.J. hurried to where it had fallen between two rocks beside the whitewater river. The light beam shot into the night sky, showing fast-falling snowflakes.

D.J. snatched up the light and flashed it quickly over the water and down the river. "Alfred? Where are you?"

There was no answer. Desperately, D.J. threw the light's beam along both banks and back to the water. But he saw nothing except the wild river surging past.

Feeling new fear, D.J. scrambled over the smooth river stones, being careful so he wouldn't plunge into the foaming water or drop the flashlight.

"Alfred?" he called, stopping where he had seen his friend extending the tree limb toward the man in the boiling pool under the falls.

There was no answer. Again, D.J. snapped the beam in every direction.

It skimmed over the water which had earned the name of Mad River. The light flipped along the far bank, leaping from rock to rock, boulder to boulder, stump to stump. Nothing!

D.J. snapped the light back to the riverbank where he stood panting in the night. His mouth was dry from a terrible fear.

There was no sign of the man and no sign of Alfred. D.J. saw nothing but fast-falling snowflakes.

D.J. slanted the light downstream. When the water left the pool, it surged into whitewater rapids. Probably nothing could live long in that short, violent section of half-submerged boulders and leaping sprays of foaming blue-green water.

About a hundred yards downstream, beyond the light's end, D.J. knew the stream leveled out to a deeper, quieter, fast-flowing current. He hurried along the bank, holding the light so it would penetrate the darkness. He stopped only where the water rounded a curve in the granite walls of Devil's Slide Canyon and there was no more trail.

D.J. started back upstream along the bank, flashing the light over the water. About fifty yards back from the curve, the light glistened on something.

"Awww!" D.J. moaned at recognizing two pieces of tree limb rocking over a couple of submerged boulders. That was the stick Alfred had been reaching out with to save Sky. The two pieces were caught by the swiftly-moving current. They raced downstream and out of sight along the curve.

D.J. tried not to think about it. But he knew that when the branch broke, it might have thrown Alfred into the swiftly moving river. Maybe the man and boy had held the stick together at that moment and had been swept downstream.

It was no use! D.J. sagged, breathing hard, his chest aching with exertion and despair.

Just a few minutes ago, Alfred had been OK. Now he was gone without a trace. So was Sky.

Unconsciously, D.J. let the light slip. The beam hit a small eddy* behind a half-submerged cottonwood stump. Something winked at D.J. from the water line. He took a couple of quick steps and held the light closer. A pair of thick eyeglasses reflected back at him.

"Alfred's glasses!"

One lens was under the water. D.J. reached down and picked up the glasses by the piece that went over Alfred's ear. D.J. straightened up, staring in horror and disbelief at what he held in his hands.

Slowly, feeling sick inside, D.J. slipped his best friend's glasses into a coat pocket.

His legs crumpled. He sank weakly upon a large smooth boulder by the river's edge and snapped off the flashlight. In the sudden darkness, D.J. heard the river gurgling by. He felt heavy snowflakes falling silently, faster and faster, upon his bare head.

Blackness such as D.J. had never known settled over him. He let his head sink heavily to his knees. His whole body shook and it wasn't from the cold.

Chapter Twelve

THE TRUTH ABOUT THE WHITE RACCOON

D.J. tried to pray, but he could not. His closed eyes were scalding with unshed tears. His mouth was dry. His heart stuck in the back of his throat. He could hardly swallow. His chest hurt as if a boulder was slowly settling upon it.

Then D.J. heard something. At first, it was so faint he didn't really notice through his pain. But the sound grew louder. It came closer.

It was a familiar sound; a chirr, yet not shrill like a grasshopper's trill. It was softer and deeper. D.J. had heard such chirring countless times, yet somehow this was different.

He slowly opened his eyes and brushed a gloved hand across the hot tears that had burned partway down his right cheek.

A little while ago, the night had been as black as any D.J. had ever seen. But now there was a faint glow everywhere. Enough snow had fallen so that the earth, brush, rocks, and limbs shimmered with a strange light.

This was a sight the boy had seen with every new snowfall. He had decided long ago that it must be the moon somehow filtering through the gray clouds with just enough light to make the whole earth seem alive. Everything glowed with a pale, strange, yet beautiful light.

Then part of the whiteness moved against the blackness of the night.

D.J. blinked and sat upright. That wasn't possible! Snow couldn't move! But it happened again!

He picked up the flashlight and snapped it on. The end of the beam reflected a pair of animal eyes that glowed like live coals.

The boy stared, seeing only the eyes. Then, against the new-fallen snow, he made out the shape of an animal.

"The white raccoon!"

D.J. whispered the words in disbelief. A legend had become real in front of his eyes!

Or was it?

D.J. clicked the light off and let his eyes again adjust to the darkness. At first, a brightness in his eyes kept him from seeing. But he heard the chirring sound again and then his eyes adjusted to the night. He couldn't see the raccoon's eyes, but he saw the animal move.

D.J. snapped the light back on. The albino raccoon *was* real! The eyes reflected brightly back. The light beam showed the ringed tail and the familiar mask on the animal's face, yet there was a difference.

The tail rings were pale; almost a tan color. The

face mask was not black, but a light blond. The rest
of the head, body, and tail were as white as any albino
could be.

For a moment, the marvel of the moment
overcame D.J. and he whispered, "Alfred, it's the white
raccoon! See?"

Then the terrible truth hit D.J. and the cruel pains
of loss ripped through his heart. He sank again upon
the rock. The flashlight sagged and the lens landed
in the soft new snow.

D.J. closed his eyes to keep back the hot tears that
threatened to burn through his head. It was so unfair!
The legendary raccoon was alive and Alfred was
dead!

The chirring sound came again. D.J. ignored it,
his mind jumping back through the times he and
Alfred had heard that special noise raccoons make.
Once the boys had seen a whole family of raccoons
coming out of a tree. Alfred and D.J. had thought
about taking one of the younger raccoons for a pet, but
they decided against it.

D.J. forced the good memory away and opened his
eyes. The white raccoon was only a few feet away.

D.J. picked up the flashlight and snapped the
beam onto the albino. Its eyes reflected the light. Then
the animal turned away and moved uphill through
the new snow. D.J. saw the familiar paw prints left
behind. They were almost like a child's handprint in
the snow.

D.J. didn't move. The albino turned back, his eyes
blazing brightly.

"Go away!" the boy said. "You didn't exist while
Alfred was alive! I don't want to see you without him!"

The raccoon's small mouth opened and the animal called again. D.J. stood up abruptly and waved his hand. "Go on! Shoo!"

The ringtail moved away a few feet then stopped, looking back at D.J. The boy stamped his feet against the ground to scare the raccoon away. It drew its legs under its body as though to run, but it didn't.

The boy took a step toward the raccoon. It turned, and again waddled slowly up the hill away from the river.

D.J. stopped. So did the albino.

A funny feeling began at the back of the boy's neck. He felt the short hairs there begin to crinkle and raise, like the hair on a dog's back when it's frightened.

D.J. took another step toward the albino. The flashlight's beam showed the snowflakes falling faster and harder. The raccoon turned away.

The boy stopped. The white ringtail turned to face him in the snow.

Shivers ran down D.J.'s neck, across both shoulders, and on down his arms. He felt goosebumps leaping up over his chest and legs.

It's almost as if he wants me to. . . . D.J. broke off his thoughts. *Naw! That's crazy!*

Still, after a moment's pause, D.J. found himself taking a step toward the rare animal. It turned and moved away, not running, not trying to escape, but staying just about the same distance from D.J. It moved inland as before, leaving dainty prints in the snow.

Gooseflesh was crawling up and down D.J.'s arms when the raccooon scrambled up a small downed sugar pine log. The boy's flashlight caught the glowing eyes for a moment, then the animal jumped down the other side of the log. D.J. saw the dry boughs move, then stop.

He stepped upon the log and flipped the light around. The paw prints led into the darkness. D.J. lifted the beam, following the prints, looking for the white raccoon.

It was gone! The tracks simply stopped as though the albino had vanished into the night air!

But just beyond the log D.J. saw something sprawled in the snow. He tipped the flashlight toward it. Then he sucked his breath in hard.

"ALFRED!"

D.J. yelled in glad surprise. He ran forward to bend over his best friend. Alfred's clothes were wet. A big bump showed through the hair plastered against his forehead. He looked different without his thick glasses.

D.J. knelt in the snow and tucked the flashlight under his left arm so the light shone in Alfred's face. Quickly, D.J. reached for Alfred's wrist to check for a pulse.

As D.J. lifted his friend's hand, a weak voice said, "I see you got my note. What took you so long?"

"You're *alive!*" D.J. jumped up and pulled off his coat to throw over his friend.

"Of course, I'm alive! Got a terrible headache, though. Slipped on a rock after I crawled out of the river and cracked my head when Sky chased me. Must have passed out."

D.J. tucked the coat around his friend. "You're soaking wet! This will keep you from freezing!"

"Good thing you came along," Alfred said, his teeth chattering. "I could've died here. I fell in the river trying to save that Sky guy."

D.J. suddenly remembered the man. D.J. snapped the light around. "Where is he now?"

"Over there." Alfred's hands moved weakly up the hillside.

D.J. flipped the beam past the brush and trees away from the river. Something reflected off of metal. D.J. stopped the light. A belt buckle sparkled weakly about six feet up in the air. A strand of wire glistened from the top of a young fir tree. In the noose end, Durant Skiver hung upside down between sky and earth.

D.J. stared. "He's caught in one of his own snares!"

"Serves him right," Alfred said with a soft chuckle.

The man called, "Get me down! You hear?"

D.J. stood up and smiled. "We'll call the deputies and *they* can get you down!" D.J. tucked the flashlight under his left armpit and cupped his hands.

"Brother Paul! Corporal Brackett! Deputy Hubble! Help! HELP!"

There was an answering call from the trees. Several lights flashed up the hill to the boys' left. D.J. aimed his light toward the men. "Over here! Hurry! Alfred's been hurt."

D.J. bent over his friend again. "You'll be OK, Alfred! They're coming! Thank God, everything's going to be OK!"

*   *   *   *   *

It wasn't long before everyone huddled around a big black heating stove in the small cabin where Sky

had kept Cletus. Sky sat in handcuffs against one
wall. Alfred was bundled warmly near the stove.
Corporal Brackett had used his handset to radio for
a helicopter to pick Alfred up in the morning. Cletus
had already given his statement to the officers. Now
it was Alfred's turn.

The deputy poised his pen over a notepad. "Start
from the beginning, please, Alfred."

"You found my note," he began. He explained that
he'd recognized Cletus' picture from a milk carton.
Seeing Sky alone in town, and not realizing the
kidnapped boy was inside the poolhall, Alfred decided
to take his dogs and go rescue Cletus from Devil's
Slide Canyon.

"It was a dumb thing to do," Alfred continued. He
pushed his eyeglasses higher on his nose. "I mean,
going down there by myself, knowing Sky was a
child-stealer.

"Anyway, Sky caught me in the woods with my
dogs. He tied them up behind the cabin and me inside
with Cletus here."

Everyone looked at the kidnapped boy, who
nodded in agreement.

Corporal Brackett finished making notes and
looked up at Alfred again. "Go on, please."

"Then Sky said he'd have to take me with him and
Cletus and get out of here before the law came. He said
he'd leave my dogs behind, but running loose. That
way, people would think maybe I drowned or
something, and nobody would ever really know
what happened to me."

D.J. turned to frown at Sky, but he didn't look up.

Alfred went on with his statement. "But I had

done one thing right. Before I started down here, I went into the public phone booth at the little store and called the missing kids hotline. I talked to what they call a technical assistant. He listened to what I said and promised to follow through. So even if Sky, here, had gotten away with me and Cletus, the trail would have been pretty hot."

Cletus cleared his throat. "Tell them about how you got away, Alfred."

"Well, Sky tied me up over there where he is now. But when all of you were trying to find the cabin, and one of you accidentally set off the trip wire alarm system—"

Deputy Hubble grinned sheepishly and petted the broad head of his Rottweiler scent dog. "*I* did that."

"Good thing," Alfred said with a grin. "When that happened, and Sky slipped outside to investigate, Cletus untied me.

"Actually, I had already gotten one hand free while Mr. Skiver—or Sky—was in the cabin. So I took a flashlight and eased out the door to try escaping. I got to the riverbank and hid. I could hear all of you men and D.J. in the distance. I wanted to call out, but in the darkness I didn't know how close Sky was to me, so I didn't dare make any noise.

"Then Sky found D.J. and I heard them running through the darkness. After awhile, I couldn't hear anymore."

D.J. said, "I think I know what happened then."

Corporal Brackett nodded but said, "Please let Alfred finish his statement."

"I was hiding by the river when I heard Sky fall into that deep pool, but I couldn't let him drown. So I held a pole out to him. He grabbed it, but when I tried to pull him in, the limb broke. I fell in.

"The current caught us both and swept us downstream. The water at the curve in the river swung us both back to the shore. Would you believe Sky grabbed up a club and started chasing me? I ran back up this way—wet, freezing, slipping and sliding in the snow. . . . "

D.J. interrupted. "I thought you'd drowned, Alfred. I had seen you trying to save Sky, and then when I couldn't find you or him—"

The corporal glanced at D.J. and he stopped in mid-sentence.

Alfred finished his story. "I guess Sky was so anxious to catch me that he forgot about setting that snare. Anyway, he got caught in it. But before I could call out to all of you, I slipped in the snow and cracked my head. You know the rest."

For the first time, Brother Paul spoke. His deep rumbling voice filled the little cabin. "Now if you all don't mind, I think it's time we said 'thanks' to our Lord for the way this all turned out."

D.J. felt all warm inside. He nodded and bowed his head.

* * * * *

A few days later, D.J. and Alfred were sitting in Brother Paul's sedan. It was parked on the shoulder of the rural road next to the little creek where the Dillons used to live before Dad and Two Mom got married.

The sun was shining on about ten inches of new snow. Almost all the oak trees and the few cottonwoods seemed to have a skirt of broken limbs

on the ground. The weight of the heavy wet snow
had piled up and snapped the strong boughs.

But the whole world was beautiful and clean and
bright. Alfred was a hero; everyone said so. He'd
helped save Cletus. People said D.J. had saved
Alfred's life. D.J. was glad Alfred was alive.

D.J. hummed happily and lowered his pencil to
the lined notepad in his lap.

Alfred looked up from his book. "Thought of
another one, D.J.?"

He nodded, writing quickly. "How about those
men from church building Grandpa's house for him?
Isn't that worth counting?"

Alfred turned to look across the creek. The sound
of hammering came clearly through the crisp autumn
air.

"Sure is! Brother Paul says that the men expect to
have your grandfather's house ready before
Thanksgiving."

D.J. nodded, thinking how strange it was that the
"new" house would be exactly like the old one where
he had lived for so long when his mother was alive.
But then, was it really so strange? That reminded him
of something.

"Stranger!" D.J. exclaimed, scribbling again. "I'm
counting Grandpa's new dog! Two Mom said Stranger
could stay with us until Grandpa's house is ready.
Now he's got a companion and that stray's got a
home."

The boys were silent a moment as D.J. reviewed a
list of good things in his life. It was surprising how
many blessings there were, and yet D.J. had almost
forgotten them.

He exclaimed, "Alfred, Brother Paul's right! If you look down at the mud of trouble, you sure can't be looking up and counting God's stars!"

Alfred grinned. "Sure looks different today from what it did a few days ago! Sky's in jail and Cletus is back with his parents. My dog and my little brother's dog are fine, and I've got you for a friend. And I'm not one of those missing children even though I had a close call. Hey! Maybe I should make my own blessing list, like you!"

D.J.'s pencil moved again. "I'm going to list my stepsister and Two Mom too. I never had a sister before, and even though Pris is sometimes a pain, she's really pretty nice. So is Two Mom."

Alfred nodded and changed the subject. "You know, I've been reading everything about legends and rare animals and so forth. There are some pretty wild stories about legendary creatures."

D.J. glanced at his friend. "Anything as strange as how I saw that white raccoon and found you?"

Alfred shook his head. "That's so unbelievable that I'm glad you decided not to tell the deputies about it."

"I didn't figure they'd believe me. And to tell the truth, Alfred, sometimes I'm not even sure it really happened. Yet I *know* it did."

"It's not logical at all," his friend admitted. "But I believe you."

"Still, I think it should be our secret—at least for awhile. Don't you?"

Alfred grinned. "I don't know. Can any writer ever keep from telling about such a thing?"

D.J. smiled and lightly touched his friend on the

shoulder. "Tell you what I'll do, Alfred. I'll write it up for the local newspaper and let the editor decide. If he believes it's true and prints it, then everyone'll know about the white raccoon and Cletus and Sky and how you got involved. But if the editor doesn't believe it, I'll put the story in a drawer and save it. Maybe someday I'll try selling it to a magazine."

Alfred shook his head. "Nope, D.J., it won't work! If it was published, we'd just be laughed at. Nobody's going to believe what really happened! And that's too bad—because I know what you could call that story."

"What?"

" 'The Legend of the White Raccoon.' "

"I like it!" D.J. exclaimed, writing it down on his pad.

"Let's hope nobody ever catches that albino. It's a cinch we can't even try after what it did for us."

"That's for sure. Too bad nobody'll ever believe it," D.J. said, chewing on the pencil eraser. "But then, you and I know it's true, so what difference does it make how others think?"

"Yeah," Alfred said with a happy grin. "It'll be our secret!"

The two friends grinned happily at each other as the sound of building continued across the creek.

LIFE IN STONEY RIDGE

BAWL-MOUTH HOUND: A hunter's term for a trail hound that bays loudly with enthusiasm while following the quarry's scent.

BLACK AND TAN: A trail hound with a black back and body, tan legs, and touches of brown, especially above his eyes.

BUGLE-MOUTH: A hunter's term for a hound with a rare baying voice that is so good it is said to sound like a bugle.

BULL PINE: Another name for a ponderosa pine. Because of unfavorable growing conditions, a bull pine usually doesn't stand more than 75 feet tall. A bull pine has hard, dark bark with deep furrows.

CARBIDE: The type of light usually found on a coal-miner's hard hat. The light comes from mixing water and gray-colored carbide pellets in a closed container, which makes a gas. This gas is released through a small hole into the reflecting chamber, which is mounted on the hard hat. A spark from a flintwheel ignites the gas and creates the light.

CHOKE-SETTER: A lumberman who prepares downed trees for the heavy equipment that will take the trees out of the woods. The choke-setter digs a hole or tunnel under the downed tree trunk. Then he throws a strong steel cable over the log and pulls it back through the hole. He puts the knob on one end of the cable through a loop on the other end and pulls the cable tight around the log. A tread-type tractor then hooks onto the log and pulls it out of the woods.

CODE THREE: An emergency; a law enforcement officer's use of the red lights and siren on his speeding patrol car. In many law enforcement agencies, including Timbergold County's Sheriff's Department, use of Code Three is authorized by the station dispatcher. But in the California Highway Patrol, use of Code Three is decided by individual officers.

CONIFERS: Another name for the many cone-bearing trees or shrubs. Spruce, fir, and pine trees are all conifers.

CORD: A measure of firewood totaling 128 cubic feet. One cord equals a stack of wood 4 feet high, 8 feet long, and 4 feet wide.

EDDY: A current that flows differently from the main stream of water. An eddy usually has a whirling motion.

EYETEETH: An expression which means a person will give anything in exchange for a desired object.

GREEN CHAIN: As freshly cut trees are sawed and turned into boards at the lumber mill, the boards fall onto a chain conveyor belt. This belt carries the green, heavy boards to be stacked before going into the kiln for drying.

HAIR-PULLING BEAR DOG: A small, quick dog of mixed breed. A hair-puller's natural tendency is to go for the heels or backside of any animal, including sheep, cows, or bears. This mutt is also called a "heeler" or "cut-across" dog.

HORNSWOGGLED: Another way of saying that someone has been lied to or fooled.

IRISH SHILLELAGH (pronounced "Shuh-**LAY**-Lee"): A cudgel or short, thick stick often used for a walking cane. A shillelagh is usually made of blackthorn saplings or oak and is named after the Irish village of Shillelagh.

LIQUIDAMBAR: A member of the sweetgum family, this slender tree is wide at the bottom and tapers up to a pointed top. The star-shaped leaves turn magnificent shades of red and yellow each autumn before falling.

MADRONE: A beautiful evergreen tree that grows to a height of about 80 feet. The pinkish-orange hardwood makes excellent firewood, though it usually doesn't split as evenly as oak does.

MAUL: A heavy hammer that often has a wooden head. A maul is used to drive a wedge into a hard piece of wood to split it.

'NAM: A short form of the name of Vietnam, a country in southeastern Asia. Vietnam was the site of American military action in the late 1960s and early 1970s.

OL' NICK: A folk name for the devil.

PIGMENT: A substance in the cells of plants or animals that gives them color.

PONDEROSAS: Large North American trees used for lumber. Ponderosa pines usually grow in the mountain regions of the West and can reach heights of 200 feet. The ponderosa pine is the state tree of Montana.

ROACH BACK: This term refers to a hump or high curve in an animal's back.

STEEL CUT OATS: The only type of oatmeal in which heat is not used in making, preparing, and packaging the product. Steel cut oats must be heated before they can be eaten.

STETSON: A broad-brimmed, high-crowned felt hat like a cowboy's. The Stetson is named for John B. Stetson, an American hatmaker who lived during the time of the Old West.

STRINGER: A newspaper reporter who sometimes writes for a publication. A stringer is not a member of a newspaper's regular staff of reporters.

SUGAR PINES: Largest of the pine trees. Sugar pines can grow as tall as 240 feet. They have cones that range from 10 to 26 inches long which are often used for decoration.

TREED: A hunter's expression meaning that the hounds have cornered their prey, often by driving it up a tree where it may try to hide. Or the prey might make a stand on the ground, backing up against a log, boulder, or other shelter. The hounds try to keep the treed animal from running away before the hunters arrive.

D.J. Dillon
· ADVENTURE SERIES ·

The Hair-Pulling Bear Dog
D.J.'s ugly mutt gets a chance to prove his courage.

The City Bear's Adventures
When his pet bear causes trouble in Stoney Ridge, D.J. realizes he can't keep the cub forever.

Dooger, The Grasshopper Hound
D.J. and his buddy Alfred rely on an untrained hound to save Alfred's little brother from a forest fire.

The Ghost Dog of Stoney Ridge
D.J. and Alfred find out what's polluting the mountain lakes—and end up solving the ghost dog mystery.

Mad Dog of Lobo Mountain
D.J. struggles to save his dog's life and learns a hard lesson about responsibility.

The Legend of the White Raccoon
Is the white raccoon real or only a phantom? As D.J. tries to find out, he stumbles upon a dangerous secret.

Winner Books are produced by Victor Books and are designed to entertain and instruct young readers in Christian principles.

Other Winner Books you will enjoy:
The Mystery Man of Horseshoe Bend
  by Linda Boorman
The Drugstore Bandit of Horseshoe Bend
  by Linda Boorman
The Hairy Brown Angel and Other Animal Tails
  edited by Grace Fox Anderson
The Peanut Butter Hamster and Other Animal Tails
  edited by Grace Fox Anderson
Skunk for Rent and Other Animal Tails
  edited by Grace Fox Anderson
The Incompetent Cat and Other Animal Tails
  edited by Grace Fox Anderson
The Duck Who Had Goosebumps and other Animal Tails edited by Grace Fox Anderson
The Mysterious Prowler by Frances Carfi Matranga
The Forgotten Treasure by Frances Carfi Matranga
The Mystery of the Missing Will by Frances Carfi Matranga
The Hair-Pulling Bear Dog by Lee Roddy
The City Bear's Adventures by Lee Roddy
Dooger, The Grasshopper Hound by Lee Roddy
The Ghost Dog of Stoney Ridge by Lee Roddy
Mad Dog of Lobo Mountain by Lee Roddy
The Legend of the White Raccoon by Lee Roddy